ZERO HOUR

BROTHERHOOD PROTECTORS WORLD

DESIREE HOLT

Twisted Page Press LLC

FOREWORD

To my readers:

Nothing ever happens in a vacuum. Even when I am writing, I am always influenced by outside influences, by my friends who brainstorm with me, by my readers who don't hesitate to give feedback, and by my team, who makes sure each book comes to life Properly: Margie Hager, my longtime great friend and beta reader; Frauke Spanath at Croco Designs whose covers always, always capture the mood of the story; Kate Richards, special friend and editor extraordinaire who makes my stories sing; Maria Connor, the very best Virtual Assistant on the planet; Steven Horwitz, my son who helps in so many ways.

Very special thanks go to law enforcement officer Joseph P. Trainor, for the key to the plot and all the information about Malmstrom Air Force Base. He has been an incredible source of information on most of my books for the past four years and I continue to be humbly grateful for the time he gives me and his willingness to share information. These books would not happen without him.

Many thanks to the fabulous Elle James for inviting me into her Brotherhood Protectors World. I hope to be here for a long time.

I write these books for you, my readers, hoping that you will enjoy each and every one. I look forward to "seeing" you and hearing from you. Find me here:

www.facebook.com/desireeholtauthor
www.facebook.com/desiree01holt
Twitter @desireeholt
Pinterest: desiree02holt

Google: https://g.co/kgs/6vgLUu
www.desireeholt.com

www.desiremeonly.com

Follow me on BookBub https://www.bookbub.com/search?search=Desiree+Holt

Amazon https://www.amazon.com/Desiree-Holt/e/B003LD2Q3M/ref=sr_tc_2_0?qid=1505488204&sr=1-2-ent

https://bookandmainbites.com/users/20900

Signup for my newsletter and receive a free book:
https://desireeholt.com/newsletter/

Join my reader group where we discuss my books
and have lots of special events:

https://www.facebook.com/
groups/DesireesDarlings/

Love,
Desiree

PROLOGUE

"To repeat, we are saddened to bring you the news that well-known hedge fund manager Frank Vanetti was shot and killed by an unknown assailant late last night."

Two men sat in the big room in matching leather armchairs, each holding a crystal glass of whiskey, staring at the television set. They focused on the reporter who wore a solemn expression as he delivered his latest bulletin.

"Vanetti was alone at his home on Blue Lake when he was shot, apparently preparing to take his boat out for an evening run. The assumption at this point is that he was killed by a sniper, probably hidden in the many trees surrounding the property. His body was found midmorning when he failed to show up for a business meeting and his assistant went to check on him. Again, financier Frank Vanetti is dead, killed by a rifle shot. This is a developing story we will continue to bring you updates on."

Deadshot, so nicknamed for his prowess with firearms, rose from the chair where he'd been sitting and turned off the television.

"That's enough. It's done, and that's all we care about."

"Excellent job, by the way," the man in the other armchair, known as Steel, commented. "As always."

"I took no pleasure in it." Deadshot sat down again, lifted the glass from the table beside him, and took a healthy swallow of the whiskey it contained.

"Nor do I," said Steel. "But it had to be done. We cannot afford one weak link in this chain. This project and the results are too important." He shook his head. "I don't understand what happened to him. He was so dedicated to our message and this project and looking forward to the results."

"You're right. It's as if he underwent some kind of metamorphosis. He was one of the biggest supporters of the project. His infusion of cash was just what we needed since my own was already tied up. What the hell, you know?"

"Yeah. I still don't know what happened to him."

"And by the way, thank you for taking care of it."

Deadshot sighed. "I'm just sorry it came to that. We're just lucky his involvement wasn't known to anyone but us."

"We damn well better hope that's the case," Steel

growled. "You checked his house for any notes he might have left? Looked in his laptop?"

Deadshot nodded. "All clean. Good thing most of the investment is already complete. We'll miss his money. Who would ever have imagined the man would decide to sabotage us? Especially after investing so heavily. Wonder what made him have second thoughts after all this time."

"We may never know, but at least he's out of the picture." Steel grunted. "Let's hope he's the only one who felt that way."

"I can promise you the others are all fully committed. Vanetti's death leaves a hole to fill, but you said you handled it."

"Already in the works." Steel blew a perfect smoke ring. "Beckett's finally come on board."

Deadshot's eyebrows rose nearly to his hairline. Lyle Beckett was almost as wealthy as Vanetti and even more radical. But beyond that, he had influence and power that reached far beyond Morgan's. There were people whose backing and support they'd need when they pulled this off. When, not if. "This is not a joke, right? He's refused to align himself with anyone until now."

"Because his plans were much larger than theirs. But he's just what we need and he's fully invested."

"You're a fucking miracle worker. I think I'll sleep a lot better tonight."

"We just have to make sure to keep him under

control. These guys think a checkbook automatically puts them in charge."

Gooding sighed. "True that."

They sat in silence after that, gazing out at the rolling land beyond the large house. It was raining outside, and drops spattered against the big picture windows. Inside, however, it was warm and cozy, with a fire crackling and the amber lights from the lamps lighting the room and reflecting off the polished wood floor. If only it could warm the cold place in his heart left by the betrayal, Steel thought to himself.

"How are things coming along on your end?" he asked. He had acquired the nickname because people said that's what he was made of.

"No problems. Like I said, everyone else on the list is on board and we are right on target," Deadshot, so nicknamed because that's what he'd been as a sniper, answered. "You know me. Follow the plan, cover all the details, get it done."

"Good, good. Just making sure we're ready for the next step." Steel drew a long pull on his cigar and blew perfect smoke rings. "I fixate on every little detail."

"That you do. "And you can be sure they're all covered. I did a little demonstration to show you. Want to see it?"

Steel sat upright. "Damn straight I do. You should have led with this."

Deadshot chuckled. "Just wanted to make sure I had your attention."

"You've got it now. Let's see it."

Deadshot picked up his tablet, which he'd left on the side table next to his chair, and activated a file.

Steel watched in fascination as an electronically created city came into view. Seconds later, what looked like a large bullet dived into the picture and into the city, which exploded instantly.

"Damn!" Steel stared, awestruck. "And that's how it will work in real time?"

"It is. This is only one of many simulations we did to make sure we had all the information necessary. I'd say it's time for the next stage. We should plan to start moving people out to the ranch."

"I think it's almost time," Steel agreed.

"These assholes will never know what hit them," Deadshot pointed out. "They all live in a deep comfort zone of denial, never realizing what needs to be done. And they never listen."

Steel shook his head. "I'm tired of running my mouth at them and getting nothing accomplished. It's time for action."

"We agree on that."

"I've got this place all prepped for them, so let's start moving people in small groups. We need to start their training now, so we don't run into complications. Everything in this project has to be exact and to the minute."

"I agree." Deadshot took a sip of his fine aged whiskey. "Good thing nobody knows about this place yet except you and me."

"Which is why it's owned by a shell corporation. And it's going to stay that way. The men need to be aware of that. No hint to anyone of where they are going or who owns it."

Deadshot thought for a moment. "I'll be sure they know that, and what will happen to them if it leaks. "I'll schedule them in small groups. Don't want that little town asking questions about a new group descending on them."

Steel was silent for a moment. "We'll do it so people will hardly notice. The ranchers out there have things happening all the time. We'll tell our people how to dress to blend in."

"Fine. Give me a date certain, and I'll pass along instructions about getting out here."

"All the supplies will be laid in by the end of the month so the first of next month works. I've picked a date to execute the plan. This gives us time to get everyone drilled on what to do."

"Do we need to vet them all again?" Deadshot asked. "Just to be sure?"

"Good suggestion. Better to be 100 percent safe. We can't afford any leaks." He took out his phone and tapped a message in the Notes app. "I'll get that put into motion right away."

"And no running their mouths," Deadshot reminded him.

"They know the penalty for that." Deadshot smiled. "This is the big one, Steel. The one that will forever cement our name in history."

"The country will be shocked," Steel agreed, "but maybe that's what it needs."

"I'm with you. Time to make a statement."

"And this will be a big one."

He leaned back in the chair. Anticipation raced through his blood. No one would be ignoring him after this.

CHAPTER 1

"You look too relaxed." The man standing in the bullpen, an Alcohol, Tobacco, Firearms and Explosives team member, grinned at his teammate, Terry Fordice. "Usually that's when the shit hits the fan."

"Don't tell me that," she groaned and made a face.

Terry, a topnotch ATFE agent herself, was relishing a rare moment of relaxation in the office, chatting with the other agent. She'd been immersed in an assignment with a three-man team and was taking advantage of a short lull in assignments.

He shrugged. "What can I say? It is what it is."

At that moment, as if prompted by his words, the phone on her desk rang.

"God forbid I should take a moment to enjoy myself," she joked as she picked up the receiver. "Fordice."

"It's Jaeger." The tone of voice was sharp and clipped. "In my office now, please."

"On my way." She hung up and turned to the other agent, who was grinning. "I've been summoned. And wipe that smartass look off your face."

"Jaeger?" he asked.

"Yeah. With Max Jaeger you never know if he's going to give you a medal or kick your ass. Wish me luck."

She hurried down the hallway, wondering what was up that prompted such a terse order.

Maybe whatever her boss had on his mind would challenge her and occupy her. God knew her social life was a big cipher. Ever since he had walked out of her life without looking back, she'd pretty much cut herself out of social activities. She knew she needed something to erase the painful memories that all these months later still clung to the edges of her mind. Something that would deal with Jesse Donovan's abrupt departure, but she hadn't found it yet.

One minute he was there, and things were growing between them. The next minute he was gone. Not even a goodbye. After the best night they'd had together, when she woke he was gone along with his motorcycle and every trace that he had ever been there. If she only knew why, maybe she could feel better about it.

Maybe.

At least she kept trying. If she could just block him out of her mind.

It's over. Terry's mind kept repeating that. *Over, over, over.*

But she hadn't been able to move forward yet. She kept reliving the memories of the two of them naked in bed, having the wildest sex she'd ever imagined. Or just sitting together, having quiet time, relaxed in each other's company. Or riding that big motorcycle of his, her seated in front so his hard cock, barely shielded by the denim of his fly, tried to insert itself between the cheeks of her ass. And it pissed her off. She'd never been one to let the end of a relationship wear on her.

"Night riding is great," he teased, urging her to get dressed. "But just put on that long T-shirt you sleep in when I can't talk you out of it."

"What? My ass will show and everything," she protested.

"Don't worry. I'll make sure no one sees it. Come on., It's our last night in the country."

She'd allowed herself to be talked into it, however reluctantly. They were staying outside of Washington, D.C. at a cottage a friend of hers knew about. They'd had long walks and sat in the sun and had more sex than she'd ever dreamed of, but tonight was their last night. She hated for this to end.

In the end she'd allowed herself to be talked into it, and off they went down the two-lane country road

DESIREE HOLT

devoid of any vehicles but theirs. Jesse had her sit in front of him instead of behind, pulling up the tail of the T-shirt so her bare ass rested against his fly. She could feel his thick, hard cock straining against his jeans, especially every time they hit a bump.

It was a bright moonlit night with a gentle breeze, and she felt freer than she ever had in her life. And hornier, with Jesse's dick all but wedged into the cleft between the cheeks of her ass.

"Lift up a little," he murmured in her ear, slowing down just a bit.

She did as he asked while he fumbled behind her and, in a moment, she felt the bare skin of his shaft rubbing in that cleft.

Holy shit!

The walls of her sex throbbed and vibrated, and she swore she could come just from the friction and the vibration of the bike. They rode like that for a long time, the contact driving her crazy. She couldn't even squeeze her legs together. Finally, Jesse pulled off the road into a little secluded area of trees, turned off the motorcycle, and nudged her forward until she was almost bent over the handlebars.

"Just feel," he whispered.

She heard the tearing of foil and the movement of his hands as he sheathed himself. Then, bending her even more and spreading the lips of her sex, he drove into her with a hard, fast thrust.

Oh god!

She thought she might come just from that movement alone

But once he had her in place, he turned on the motorcycle, leaving it in a low gear, the vibrations racing through their bodies. She squirmed back toward him, but he held her firmly in place, working his cock in and out while the bike did a lot of the work for them.

She was so lost in the sensations, in the orgasm building inside her, eyes closed to immerse herself in it, that when she exploded it shocked her. Jesse had one thick arm tight around her waist, clasping her to him while they shook with the force of their combined release.

When her inner walls stopped spasming and Jesse's cock stopped throbbing, she leaned forward as if she'd never be able to move again. Jesse kissed the back of her neck and stroked the cheeks of her ass before easing himself from her body. Covered again by her T-shirt she let him settle her in place and kick the bike into third gear .

She was sure she'd never forget one minute of this evening.

And she never had.

In all her other relationships, she was the one who walked away. Not this time, not the one time it mattered, and the pain kept trying to push itself back to the surface. She'd always told herself not to get invested in a relationship but with Jesse there had been an invisible connection, something that bound them together. She'd opened her heart to him as well as her body and her mind and gotten pain and betrayal for her trust.

Never again, she told herself. Never, ever again. She'd keep her emotional and mental distance from all men from now on. It was a lot less painful that way. Hopefully Jaeger would have an assignment for her that would wipe Jesse Donovan out of her mind.

Yeah. As if.

Jaeger was waiting for her, sitting on the edge of his desk rather than more formally behind it, so maybe the ass kicking wasn't on the docket. He was a tall, lean man with a weathered face who had been with ATFE for a number of years. Stories about him in the field were legend. Terry had considered it an honor and a special privilege when she was assigned to his team.

"Have a seat." He indicated one of the two chairs in front of the desk.

"Am I in trouble?" she asked at once.

"Only if you say no."

She studied his face, trying to discern if he was kidding or not.

"Okay, tell me what's up."

"We have a problem, and we're running out of solutions."

Terry lifted an eyebrow. "What kind of problem and how can I possibly solve it?"

"We've had our eye on Reed Morgan for some time. You know who he is, right?"

"Yes, I've read about him. Former military. Left the Army and opened an arms manufacturing company, which has grown to be a monster. Lots of guesses on where his financing came from. Outspoken critical of the government, which he calls too liberal."

Max rubbed his jaw. "That's the guy."

"Then yes, when I joined the ATFE I was aware he had been a priority for some time."

"Yeah, we've had our eye on him, watching his activities. The watch on him has been bumped up several notches in the past year. You know Morgan is considered a hard-liner. Among many other things, he's been lobbying hard to overturn some of the recently passed gun laws, and his disdain for the government is well-known."

"The whole agency knows Morgan Arms Manufacturing is one of the largest businesses of its kind in this country. They also own retail stores, plus they supply some of the arms to our military and even more go overseas. Lots of rebellions going on in the world. But I'm guessing you called me in here because something has pushed this to the forefront."

"It has."

"I know he's spoken loudly about what he sees as the failure of America to enforce its laws, and the subsequent rise of crime." Terry shook her head.

"About the increasing numbers of what he called 'soft' laws that barely punished the criminals. But speaking out isn't a crime, although for some people I think it should be. So, what's changed here?"

"Our sources tell us Morgan Arms is suddenly buying a lot more steel, plastic, and aluminum than usual," he told her, "so a lot of questions have floated in the air. That was the first thing that caught the director's eye."

"Has his client list increased?" Terry asked. "Have his orders from overseas clients gotten bigger?" Max rubbed his jaw. "After all, there is always a rebellion going on someplace and some army, legitimate or otherwise, that needs weapons. Or maybe they're preparing to release a newly designed instrument. Or finally, is there another reason we don't know that means trouble for everyone? I agree none of those possibilities are appealing. That's for damn sure. But buying more raw materials and railing against the government isn't a crime. If it was the jails would be full all the time."

"True," Jaeger agreed. "But here's something you don't know. For some time, Morgan's been gathering a group together, first his closest friends and then people who we think share his beliefs about the way this country is run. You know there have been attacks by these off-the-wall militia groups and, based on what we learned, we're afraid Morgan's plotting another one. Anyway, over a year ago we managed to plant someone in Morgan's group. We needed to find out what the hell was happening. He's deep undercover, and sometimes we have to wait weeks for a word from him, which doesn't help.."

"Damn!"

"No kidding. When my guy does get word out to me, he says Morgan's running this like it's the military, which is what we figured. I think Morgan's made this group his own private militia, kind of an outlaw posse comitatus. He also has three or four specially selected men who he calls his 'guard' who watch the rest of them like hawks. He's been making trips recently to the land he owns in Montana, a spread in the Crazy Mountains. Each time, he takes a few of his group with him. Our undercover got taken there once. He managed to get a message out that they train. All day. Every day. Exercise. Firearms. Hand-to-hand combat. And they study explosives."

"Explosives."

"Yeah, but they don't actually detonate anything. I'm sure the neighbors would complain."

"Still... Are they preparing for war?"

"That's what we need to know. And it's been a while since our guy communicated with us."

"He must be in danger. If Morgan finds out who he is, he'll kill him."

"That's right. Morgan keeps those guys on a chokehold. The last word my guy managed to get to us knocks all this to the front of the line. He said something very big and very destructive is being planned. He's not in Morgan's inner circle, but he and others have been told that before long they'll be getting ready for an event that will change the country."

"My god! What do you think it is? What does the director think?" She was getting an itchy feeling about this. "What's his spread in Montana like? Could it be taking place there?"

"It's two hundred acres of prime land he bought from the neighboring ranch that itself stretches ten thousand acres. I understand the entire perimeter of Morgan's place is fenced, and he has a state-of-the-art security system at the ranch house."

"Paranoid much?" she snarked.

"Not only that, that entire area is snugged up right to the foothills of the Crazies. They provide a great barrier, so people can't spy on him."

"Wonderful. Just great. For him."

"There are some options, but they aren't being used, mostly because the ranches on either side like it that way, and people are afraid of getting shot if they do. They're training for something that's in the works. Word is it won't take place there because there's no logical target. Malmstrom Air Force base is located nearby at Great Falls, but it's impossible to get on there and plant explosives. Besides, it would not make a big enough statement."

"Blowing up a military facility?"

"Our guy seems to think Morgan is aiming for something bigger."

Terry frowned. "And you believe your guy is passing along good information?"

"I do. He was specially picked for this because he's so good at it and very reliable. We think the increased purchases of materials for gun manufacture Morgan made recently are only part of it. The second part. We know something huge is in the wind, and we have to find out what it is before it bites us in the ass and we have a disaster of epic proportions." He paused. "One other thing. A few days ago, hedge fund manager Frank Vanetti was killed. He managed resources in the billions, and it's been whispered behind tightly closed doors he's Morgan's money man. The one who financed Morgan Arms in the beginning and may be financing whatever this big episode is."

Terry tilted her head. "I guess the startup money had to come from somewhere. You don't actually leave the military with a lot of change in your pockets."

"Right." Jaeger agreed. "But if whatever he's planning is of the magnitude we fear, he would need a lot more resources than he has at his disposal."

"Okay, then who killed Vanetti? And why? Would he and Morgan have had a falling out of some kind? Why kill off the golden goose?"

"That's the question of the hour. Or questions. We

have to find the answers and it won't be easy. If Morgan's behind it only a major falling-out would cause this."

"So, what's my role in all this?"

Max studied her face for a long time before answering.

"We need someone to get real close to Morgan. We decided it should be you. Finding that answer is part of it. Glean as much info from Morgan as possible and see if you can determine what the fuck he and his friends are up to. See if you can get him to let something slip. Check on who he spends time with. I have a feeling we're on a timetable. Someone needs to connect with Morgan and see if they can find out what the hell is up, before it's too late."

"Great." Terry made a face.

"We looked at this from all angles and you should know the brass agrees with me you're perfect for this assignment. You're sharp, smart, able to think on your feet, and expert with weapons and self-defense if you need them. You also have the kind of classy appearance that means Morgan won't hesitate to include you in some of his activities. See if you can get a hint from any of those conversations."

Terry laughed. "Is that a sexist remark?"

"It's a dead serious one," he pointed out, "and I think you know it. There's a lot riding on this. What we'd like is for you to get close to Reed Morgan. We got you credentials with *American Made,* a magazine devoted to American firearms and enthusiasts. Your cover is you've been assigned by the magazine to do a profile on Reed Morgan. His life. His daily routine. The growth of his company. We want him to take you to meetings and events where he believes you'll fit in so he can show you all the public parts of his life. And hopefully in all that you'll find a clue to what the fuck is going on."

Terry laughed. "You think I can just waltz into his office, and he'll say sure, let's do it?"

"He already has." Her boss handed her a thin stack of business cards and a cell phone. The cards had Teresa Franklin on them and below it *American Made* and a phone number. "Obviously we weren't going to use your actual surname. The number goes with that phone. If he calls that number, someone here will answer and give him the answers he's looking for."

"And the magazine is fine with this?"

Jaeger nodded. "The publisher got his balls in a wringer a couple of years ago, and we bailed him out. He owes us. Now it's time to pay up."

"Just to verify, you're telling me it's all set up?"

"It is," he assured her. "It appeals to his ego. God knows he has a huge one. Get him to agree to let you follow him around, get a feel for what he does at work and outside the office."

"So, let's see. You want me to find out why the extra firearms, what the big bang is they're planning, and when it's going to take place." Terry couldn't help laughing. "Oh, and if they killed Vanetti and who pulled the trigger. You have a lot of confidence in me, Max."

"True." His face was dead serious. "We all do. You've pulled off something like this more than once. I believe you can do it again, and everyone from the director on down agrees with me. Part of this assignment is to get him to mention Frank Vanetti if you can. His connection to Morgan and his group is well hidden but we're hoping he +might let something slip. We also would like to know the name of his new money man."

"Oh, so you don't want much. Just miracles."

"Always hope for those," Jaeger told her.

Terry snorted. "Fat chance. Just from other stuff I've read, the man's more closemouthed than a dead fish."

" We'll see. Maybe we'll get lucky. Do not, however, under any circumstance bring up Vanetti's name yourself."

"Got it."

Terry felt a little flutter in her stomach, a combination of nerves and excited anticipation. If she succeeded in this assignment, it would be a huge boost to her career. She didn't even want to examine the possibilities if she failed.

"When am I supposed to start?" she asked.

"Right away." He picked up a slim folder from his desk and handed it to her. "Your homework for tonight. I didn't want to send it to your existing phone in case the wrong people got hold of it. Or to your laptop in case it got hacked."

Terry raised an eyebrow. "Hacked? You think Morgan would have someone try to dig into my laptop? I won't even have it anywhere around him."

"Doesn't matter. He's got people who can do anything. If the Russians and the Chinese can hack servers around the world, getting into your laptop would be a breeze."

She frowned. "Damn, Max. So, the guy really is that paranoid?"

"He is. Which is why you have to be extremely careful around him." He leaned a little closer. "Terry, if I didn't think you could do this job, I wouldn't be sending you." He paused. "Want to turn it down?"

"What? Hell, no. I'll get what you want. No question about it."

"If things start to go south," he told her, "or your cover is blown, get out of there at once. We can always try another angle. I'm not gambling with your life."

"I'll be fine," she assured him. "If Reed Morgan is planning something big and dangerous, I want to find out what it is so we can stop him."

"Just remember— " he started again.

She held up a hand. "Got it. Now. Details, please. I assume I'm going to San Antonio, since that's where his headquarters is?"

"Yes." He handed her an envelope. "Plane, car, and hotel reservations, and a driver's license also in the name of Teresa Franklin, to go with the business cards. I didn't want to use your last name in case Morgan has someone run a trace on you. Who knows how deep they can dig about someone."

"I agree."

He reached behind him for something else and handed her a cell phone. "A burner for when you call here. Good luck."

"I make my own," she sassed, then rose from her chair. "Thanks for having confidence in me for this."

"You've proven yourself, Terry. Just be careful."

At least she had something to occupy her mind besides thoughts of Jesse Donovan, and maybe something to fill the hole in her heart.

CHAPTER 2

TERRY SIPPED her club soda and watched Reed Morgan who was engaged in what appeared to be a casual conversation with another man. George Something. She'd written it down in her phone because George had been in two of the meetings she'd attended with Morgan. But from the attitude of both men, he didn't seem to be key to the operation. She was getting frustrated attending all these meetings and events with her subject, only getting answers to the superficial questions.

And she knew time was getting short. Max Jaeger's anonymous source had sent him a message that things were moving rapidly and whatever was going to happen, it would be within the month.

Crap. That's all she could say. Crap.

But she couldn't push without creating suspicion.

She'd been here two weeks, following him around

on her assignment as much as he'd allow, and hadn't even gotten one whiff of whatever he had planned. She was irritated and frustrated and upset with herself for not being able to complete her real assignment. But Reed Morgan was an expert at keeping an invisible wall around himself and never letting information out in conversation.

By now she could probably write Morgan's bio based on his public character, she hadn't found even a hint of what she'd been sent to learn. The man was a master at avoiding anything he didn't want to discuss, and she couldn't be too pushy or he'd get suspicious. He was, however, pleased about the so-called article and, on that front, extended her every cordiality.

The only indication he gave that something might be happening was the first day she'd met him, in his office.

"I have some exciting things planned for the future," he told her. "This article comes at just the right time. I'll have to thank the publisher."

"I consider myself lucky I got this assignment. You're quite the legend in the firearms and munitions community."

He'd just shrugged. "I've been lucky. Had some good breaks. The business has grown more than I even anticipated."

She'd wanted to say something about his increased purchasing of raw materials but didn't want to give him any reason to suspect her of anything. Why would a magazine writer know about that, anyway?

Also, there had been no mention of Frank Vanetti. Not that she'd expected it, since his association was supposedly a big secret but she'd hope someone would accidentally let something drop. She couldn't be obvious about it, but she hoped. She did text Max Jaeger and tell him they would probably have to go at that from another angle. If she found anything out it would be only by accident. She was focusing everything on finding out what the big project was.

Before arriving in the city, she'd read everything on him she could get her hands on, searching the Internet for articles and news items. She'd seen enough photos and video clips of Morgan Reed to know he wore the image of a man with a steel core. In fact, he had turned out to be exactly what she expected—a man who was focused and in charge. And had a large ego.

At forty-five he was a man who obviously worked at keeping himself in top physical shape. He seldom wore suits except for events like tonight, preferring instead soft-collared shirts and tailored slacks that showed exactly how fit he was. His square-jawed face was weathered, tanned, and topped by close-cropped brown hair threaded with gray. He looked exactly like someone who could be plotting anything from a murder to overthrowing a government and never blink until it was done. Despite the fact that he went out of his way to be pleasant to her, knowing he could be planning something disastrous sent chills down her spine, shivers that she worked hard to conceal.

On the surface, though, things were progressing nicely. She had given him the story Jaeger had told her to use that her editor wanted her to spend a couple of weeks or more in San Antonio. Get a feel for what he did on a regular basis. Accompany him as much as possible without disturbing his responsibilities. Pick up on anything that would round out the profile on him and make it a better article.

"You're an icon of the industry," she told him. "That's why this is going to be the cover story, and we want to get it right."

Apparently, however, he wanted this article to develop in a certain way. She'd spent a day touring Morgan Arms Manufacturing, impressed with the size of the operation and learning to test a weapon on the firing range. When he admired her expertise with a weapon, he seemed satisfied with her explanation that she'd had a boyfriend who was military and taught her. She figured it was better than trying to hide it and getting caught unexpectedly.

When she told him she'd like to talk to some of his closest friends, kind of round out the picture of him, he had no objections. In fact, he set up a dinner where she could meet them and explain what she was looking for.

"Got to butter them up so they'll say good things about me," he'd joked at the time.

Five people had joined them at the restaurant, including the man he introduced to her as his closest friend, Ed Gooding, who was there with his wife Nita. As soon as she shook hands with the woman, Terry's antennae began waving, and she marked Nita as someone to be on the alert about. The tiny flare of jealousy in the other woman's eyes when she learned the purpose of the visit was an indication of where Nita stood on this. But then she'd smiled and donned her cordial face.

She hoped someone would mention the death of Frank Vanetti, but it never came up. It would have been awkward for her to introduce it, but it frustrated her just the same.

During the days that followed, she sometimes found herself in other social situations with the woman. Morgan had Terry accompany him to all of his public activities. Knowing what she did, she had a feeling he was building an image for her that would help once whatever he planned hit the front pages. Maybe be a platform for his particular beliefs.

When Morgan brought her to gatherings like this, telling her he wanted her to see both the business and pleasure sides of his life, more often than not the Goodings were also there.

Terry had perfected that art of subtle questioning, which was another reason Max Jaeger had picked her for this assignment. She was pretty sure Ed Gooding wasn't the new money man. He was too visible. But she did peg him as Morgan's lieutenant in whatever group he had formed and whatever he was planning. And as such Gooding was also very good at answering questions without giving information.

There was one particular thing she'd been on the lookout for, although Max Jaeger had assured her it would not be a problem. In situations like this there was always the possibility the subject would hit on her. She wasn't vain, but she knew she was an attractive woman, especially when she took pains with her hair and makeup. She was relieved when Morgan made no move on her at all.

You just never knew in an environment like this how it would go, and she'd had to deal with it before.

There didn't seem to be a steady woman in his life, but men like Reed Morgan didn't waste emotion on people. She supposed when he had an itch to scratch he found a willing and discreet woman.

Thank god he hadn't expected her to fall into that category. Morgan was a professional all the way, even if that professional might be plotting to endanger the country. She was relieved to discover that he was a man who separated business and pleasure and obviously wasn't about to do anything to screw this up.

Instead, he'd been welcoming, his ego obviously

stroked by the prospect of the featured article in the premier arms magazine, *American Made*. It appealed to him in a way not many other things might have. It made setting up a good relationship with him much easier than she'd expected. Although he was a naturally suspicious man, he also had an ego a mile wide. He'd want people to know who he was and what he stood for. Create a persona people would admire. Max Jaeger had been right about that. Terry was sure he had his own agenda regarding this.

She learned Morgan was also a man who liked to control the world around him, and as she got to know him she realized he knew exactly how to push people's buttons to achieve that. When he'd agreed to have her shadow him so she could get a full picture of him, that had involved attending events like this one tonight. Part of her undercover assignment was to assess the people at these gatherings, see who spent time talking to Reed, who he might focus on. And, if possible, do a little eavesdropping.

Of course, as Terry kept telling herself, whatever he was planning, he wasn't about to discuss it or even hint at it around her. She tried as much as possible each time to see if she could casually snap a picture of whomever he was chatting with. Sometimes, however, she'd turn for a moment to answer a question and, when she'd look back, he'd have disappeared from the room. Too bad she couldn't go searching for him without sparking all kinds of questions and arousing his suspicions because she was damn sure whatever he was talking about with someone had to do with her reason for being here.

Still, using the nifty little camera pin Jaeger had outfitted her with, she managed discreetly to get photos of some of the people. After she went back to her hotel, she'd email them to the office.

One thing she noticed, and had to admire, was the way he sidestepped issues he didn't want to address. She'd tried to question him about the effect arms-control protests and proposed laws had on his business. How he handled the names people sometimes called him or the constant stream of proposed gun-control laws. But Morgan was as adept at sidestepping questions as he was at running his business. Half the time she didn't even know she'd been finessed, which was saying something.

If there was anything that irritated her it was the continued presence of Curt Renshaw. He was a silent but almost threatening presence wherever they went. At small gatherings she would move away from the immediate area, but you always knew he was there, somewhere, waiting. She'd give anything to know the reason for him being there. Morgan himself was no pushover, so there must be some serious threats out there. But, she wondered, which side of the fence did they come from?

Ostensibly he was Morgan's driver, ferrying them everyplace. In reality, though, she'd come to realize he was Morgan's personal bodyguard. She wondered whether he'd pissed off so many people he needed protection or if Renshaw was part of the militia they'd heard so much about and protected Morgan from people who violently objected to his beliefs. He was a quiet presence wherever they went, discreetly placing himself in the background but always on alert.

She was reminded of the term *eminence gris*— a person who exercises power or influence in a certain sphere without holding an official position. She wondered just how much power Renshaw actually had. She'd managed to capture a picture of him and send it to Max with a request for information. So far all she'd learned was he was exactly what she thought —a bodyguard with a lot of power. But she wanted to know his background and just how he and Morgan had become such tight asshole buddies.

In all the conversations, either between her and Morgan or with others, while she'd listened carefully for any mention of Frank Vanetti, there had been none. Max Jaeger had warned her not to bring the name up herself since it might be a hot button and make Morgan suspicious. Their connection was not known except to a tiny circle of intimates, but she kept hoping it would come up in conversation. No such luck. She kept hoping something someone said would trigger a mention, but so far nothing. When she subtly questioned him about his friends, looking for clues, he mentioned the Goodings and two other couples but no Vanetti. And when she'd asked hm if Morgan Arms Manufacturing had any partners, he quickly shut her down, telling her he liked total control.

Tonight was yet another one of the gatherings he'd told her he was obligated to attend. Sometimes they were purely social, but usually they had a purpose. Raising money for some community need or some scholarship program or planning how to handle the latest upsurge in gun-control protests and proposed laws. The people on this guest list, as with the others, all had two things in common—they were filthy rich and controlled a lot of power.

At the moment, this party was in full swing, the hum of multiple conversations overlaying each other filling the air. Bowing to the pleasant temperature outside, the doors to the covered patio were open, and some people had chosen to move out there to chat. A server quietly circulated in both areas with a tray of hors d'oeuvres. Morgan circulated the large room, smoothly identifying people he wanted to connect with. Answering her questions about the extent he wished to be involved in this latest project. She knew he was quietly trying to assess how much money he'd commit to it.

At the moment, he was in deep conversation with a man he had yet to introduce her to.

"Give us a second, will you?" he asked. "This won't take long."

He didn't explain why he needed to speak to the man alone or even introduce him. She tried to ease closer to the group he was in to see if she could overhear anything being said, but the big room was crowded, and there was too much ambient noise. Then the other man gave a short jerk of his head and the two of them slipped out the sliding glass doors to the patio. If she followed, it would be much too obvious, especially with Renshaw stuck to them like a barnacle. Morgan was very good at giving her the slip when he wanted privacy, and she was still working to find a way around that without creating suspicion. Maybe she could ease closer to the open patio door. She glanced around to see where Renshaw was and realized he had gone outside with Morgan. Interesting.

She had just refilled her glass of club soda at the bar when a man in one corner of the huge room caught her eye and she blinked, sure she was hallucinating. He was tall and lean, with midnight-black hair tamed into place and a well-groomed scruff beard. The sport jacket and slacks fit him as if they'd been tailormade for his toned body. A sharp pain stabbed her at the sight and for a moment she stopped breathing. No. No, no, no. She was wrong. It couldn't be him. What would Jesse Donovan be doing here, anyway? This was definitely not his cup of tea.

In fact, he hadn't even said goodbye just left before she even got up.

She hated that the former had suddenly popped up in her memory banks after months of trying to keep him in a dark corner. The last time she'd been with him he wasn't looking for company of any kind, hers or anyone else's. Leaving the SEALs hadn't worked out well for him and he hadn't wanted "some well-meaning do-gooder" trying to help solve his problems and arrange his life. She'd been a lot more than that to him, or at least she'd thought she was. Thought they'd actually been a lot to each other. Apparently she was the only one who felt that way because he dropped out of her life as if he'd never even been there. She hadn't seen him or heard from him in three years, and it shocked her that out of the blue someone reminded her of him.

This is crazy. I have got to stop this.

She blinked again, and the man came more sharply into focus. Not Jesse. Someone else. But someone who clearly resembled him. She didn't know if she was relieved or disappointed. But the ache was still lodged in her chest, damn it.

"Enjoying yourself?" Morgan spoke quietly in her ear.

His voice startled her, mostly because she'd been so preoccupied staring at the stranger she hadn't even noticed him come back into the room, much less heard him come up behind her. She'd need to pay better attention. He rested a hand on her shoulder, lightly, not aggressively, but she knew that he was sending a signal to everyone. As he had at all the other gatherings, he wanted people to know that she was here with him. Not as his "date," but as someone important. Whatever her role in his life, he was letting everyone else know they'd better stand back.

She turned and gave him her practiced smile. "Of course I am. I have to say, Reed, I'm very impressed with the people who form your circle of friends."

He snorted. "Most of these people are only friends as long as I keep up with them financially and have something to offer them. And with each one it's something different. They're also a little envious of what I do, the perceived roughness of my business. It's amazing how the rough edge of life entices them"

She lifted an eyebrow. "That just seems to out of character for them."

"It is, and probably why it appeals to them so much." He barked a short laugh. "Believe me, they'd love it if I gave them the brutal details of uprisings in Africa or rebels in South America. Of course, they'd never actually get close to any of it. Too nasty and too dangerous. But they like cozying up to me and then telling their weak-assed friends what a badass I am."

Terry laughed. "I'm sure they'd be disappointed to know your opinion of them."

"They don't care as long as they get to rub elbows

with what they think of as the rougher side of life. And I don't care as long as they cut political red tape for me. Why don't I get you another drink?"

"I'm good. I'll just keep nursing this one." She had managed so far to get her own drinks at these events and to nurse one glass of wine if she was with him at a dinner.

"Evening, Reed." Lyle Beckett moved over to where they were standing. His voice was deep with a slight gravelly sound.

Terry had been introduced to him at another event and told he was the head of a hedge fund. That had perked up her interest. Was this the replacement for Frank Vanetti? Hedge fund owners could move vast amounts of money around at will and cover their tracks so well it would take a big shovel to dig deep and find the truth of transactions. Besides that, however, the little niggle that she'd seen him somewhere before grew in size as she stood next to him. But where the hell would she have seen him? And how? She needed to ask her boss about this, fighting the sudden feelings that whatever it was would not be good.

Prejudiced much, Terry?

Maybe, but she'd been involved with enough people like that to be able to get a good sense of them. The night she'd met him, he and Morgan had greeted each other but spent little time chatting. Was that deliberate? To her suspicious mind that could mean they didn't want her to think they were intimately connected.

Morgan smiled and held his hand out to the other man. "Good to see you here."

Beckett grunted an acknowledgement then shifted his gaze to Terry.

"Nice to see you again, Miss Franklin. Hope you're enjoying yourself."

His gaze raked over her from shoulders to shoes. She had the feeling he could see right through her skin, which creeped her out, but she just smiled and nodded. "It's all very interesting."

Beckett turned back toward Morgan, an obvious dismissal of her.

"Sorry to interrupt you, Reed. I just need your ear for a few minutes. I wouldn't bother you if it wasn't important. I promise not to keep you long."

Beside her, Morgan tensed, and his fingers tightened for a brief second on her shoulder. Then he nodded at the other man.

"Of course." He glanced at Terry. "Think you'll be okay if I step outside again for a few?"

"Absolutely I'm meeting a lot of interesting people here. Helps me flesh out your profile. Take your time."

She smiled and fiddled with the pin on her blouse, managing to snap some quick shots of Lyle Beckett.

"Don't let anyone try to talk you into doing a profile on them," he joked.

"No problem." She smiled at him. "All my focus is on you."

In more ways than one.

"I'll be right back." He turned to Beckett. "Let's walk out on the patio. There are a few people out there but also some private areas."

They moved unhurriedly through the crowd, smiling at people as they eased past them.

Terry stared after them for a moment, wondering why Beckett seemed familiar. She knew she'd remember if she'd ever met him before

Looking casually around, she saw Nita Gooding huddled at the other side of the room with a small group and for a change not focusing on her. This might be her chance to pick something up. She waited for a count of five before edging her way toward the open glass doors. The way the room was set up there was a little jut in the wall at one end of the sliding door that she could just fit into. Standing there, she would be hidden from outside and hopefully could overhear some of Morgan's conversation. She had a feeling, of all the people she'd met in the past couple of weeks, this one played a key role in whatever Morgan had planned.

She was sipping her drink and pretending to study something in an app on her watch when she caught bits and pieces of Morgan's conversation.

"Tell them that's the way it is. If they don't fucking

like it, then they're finished. And you know what that means."

"What I said. If we have to eliminate someone, so be it. This thing is so big we don't have any wiggle room."

"Country will be talking about this for a long time." A short laugh. "At least, whoever's left."

"Can't afford any slipups. Need to head for Montana tomorrow. I'll finish up this business…join you by the end of the week."

"Better get inside…"

"When it's done."

CHAPTER 3

TERRY KNEW she'd better make herself scarce before Morgan and Beckett actually walked back into the party. She eased away from where she was standing and headed toward the powder room She managed to make it the crowd to the hallway, glancing over her shoulder to see Morgan back in the big room and scanning the crowd. She turned the corner to the powder room before either man could spot her, slipped in, and closed and locked the door, letting out a breath. She was sure she'd left her listening post before Morgan saw her there, but she needed a few minutes alone to be sure she didn't look rattled when she joined the man again.

They were going somewhere, Morgan and Lyle Beckett, she'd heard that much. Somehow she had to find out, however, exactly who was going and where they were headed. Was it a gathering of the rumored militia? How many people would be there? Where would it be? What was it for? What was Beckett's role, because her well-developed sixth sense told her he was definitely involved.

And another thing.

She needed to call Max Jaeger as soon as she got back to the hotel. She'd sent him Lyle Beckett's name after their first meeting but without any note attached. Tonight she wanted to add her impression of the man plus include the picture. Although she had little enough to give her boss, he was the best at digging deep and digging things out. Meanwhile, she needed to compose herself before she went back into the main area of the house. Over the course of the last couple of weeks, she'd watched how accurately Morgan read people. She needed to make sure her face was a blank.

She opened the door to the powder room and looked both ways down the little hallway. The noise of the party overflowed into it, but no one was standing there, at least for the moment. But as she headed back toward the gathering, Nita Gooding rounded the corner from that direction, apparently also on the hunt for the same thing.

Now she stared at Terry with narrowed eyes.

"Looking for something? There's nothing that way except a bathroom."

"Which is just where I'm coming from." Terry smiled and gestured toward the open door.

"Oh! Of course. How silly of me. That's right where I'm heading." She started past Terry then turned around. "You know, if Reed is busy in one of his little private talks at these shindigs, you can always come and hang out with me."

"Thank you. I'll keep that in mind. But I like to talk to the people who know Reed. You know, get a well-rounded picture of him."

"Oh?" Nita arched an eyebrow. "I was—I mean, a little while ago I saw Reed had just stepped outside for a private conversation, and I noticed you hanging out by the glass doors to the patio, looking a little lost. Were you? Lost, I mean?" Evil curiosity sparked in her eyes. "You wouldn't be trying to eavesdrop on Reed, would you? I'm not sure he'd be too happy about that."

Crap!

"Of course not." She pulled out her best professional smile. "I was just catching my breath. But thanks for asking."

She turned and walked away, but she could feel the other woman's eyes boring into her. Damn! It seemed her original sense of Ed Gooding's wife was right on target. She, Terry, needed to be more careful around her. She thought she'd done a pretty good job of blending in with people tonight and not standing out, but apparently she'd fallen short. She should have paid more attention to where Nita was in the room.

As nonchalantly as she could, she strolled back into the heart of the party where the socializing was still going strong. Her gaze landed on Lyle Beckett, who watched her with hooded eyes as if he could see right through her. A tiny chill slithered down her spine. This was a man she needed to be very careful around.

He was standing off to one side now talking to Ed Gooding. When he saw Terry, however, he broke off the conversation and walked over to her.

"Where'd you disappear to?" he asked. "I came back inside and couldn't find you."

She grinned. "Just a trip to powder my nose. So, Lyle Beckett seems like a fascinating man, although I only exchanged a few words with him. Is he involved in your business?"

Morgan narrowed his eyes slightly and studied her, as if looking for some kind of clue to her question in her expression.

"We've touched on some joint ventures before but mostly he has his own projects. You only met him for three minutes. Why all the curiosity?"

"Oh. No biggie, but like I said, he seems like he'd be interesting to talk to. In my line of work, you learn to sense things about people. I thought I would add another dimension to the profile on you."

Again, his face was like a mask. "We don't do enough together to make it worth the effort. Come on, there are some noteworthy people I haven't introduced you to yet."

Okay, then. If she was going to find out more about Lyle Beckett it would have to be through some source other than Morgan. Tonight when she sent Max Jaeger the picture of Beckett, she'd ask him to have someone do deep research on the man. Then he could let her know if she should pursue it further.

For the next hour, Terry kept a professional smile plastered on her face as they moved from group to group. The people Morgan introduced her to were what she thought of as window dressing. People who knew him as a community leader but had nothing to do with his business or anything he did off the books. If he really was planning something big, they weren't the people who'd know about it.

Lyle Beckett, on the other hand, fit the profile of people she was looking for. She'd hoped to have more time to observe him and see who he interacted with, but Morgan had an on/off switch she'd gotten used to. When he was finished with an event, he was done.

"Did you enjoy yourself?" Morgan asked once they were in his car heading away from the event.

"Of course. I enjoy meeting your friends. Helps me get a better picture of you for the profile."

He barked a short laugh. "As I've told you before, most of the people you're meeting aren't friends. They're business or community acquaintances, but they know enough to give you what you want about me."

She glanced over at him. "I haven't asked you this, but what is that you think I want?"

"I think you're looking for the fly in the ointment, as they say." He turned onto IH-10, heading downtown to where her hotel was. "Something your readers can point to and say I'm not all that."

She frowned. "That's a very cynical way of looking at things. We want this profile to tout your position in the community and your leadership in the arms-manufacturing business. My publisher chose you because he likes what you stand for."

"Yeah?" There was a long moment of silence. "Somehow we never discussed this. Exactly what does he believe that is?"

"Strength. Values. Leadership in a volatile industry. Someone who gives back to the community. Why are you asking me this? We discussed it in our first meeting, remember?"

He shrugged. "Just checking. You can't be too careful these days. I've been shot in the ass enough to know things aren't always what they seem. People have hidden agendas."

Stay calm. There's no way he could know your real assignment. No one knows except for me, Max, and a couple of DEA higher ups. Even the publisher doesn't know the real reason for this setup. It's all been kept very hush hush.

"My only agenda is to learn as much as I can abut you so I can write a profile that will make both you and my publisher happy."

"You'll have to excuse my naturally suspicious nature," he told her. "The business I'm in, believe it or not, is very cutthroat. Plus, we're always under fire, as you and I discussed, from the gun-control people and those who think we shouldn't even manufacture weapons."

"I've asked you about this before," she said, "and you kind of sidestepped the issue, but how do handle people like that? All the protests and everything."

"You met my public relations people. They're damn good at smoothing out situations. Personally, I choose not to get involved. I've learned that in situations like that whatever you say is taken out of context and used against you."

"That has to be a difficult way to live."

He was silent for so long she wasn't sure he'd say anything.

"I chose to go into a business that, pardon the pun, is often under fire, because I believe in the Second Amendment. I also believe in the rights of people to defend themselves against brutality and oppression, which is why we got involved in situations in so many other countries. Believe me, Morgan Arms Manufacturing has taken a lot of grief for arming rebels and the oppressed."

"But you're doing what you believe in," she pointed out.

"Not everyone would look at it that way." He glanced at her. "Not even our government." He pulled off the interstate and into the downtown area. "But that's a discussion for another time. Maybe. What I've been trying to show you is that we are a law-abiding corporation run by law-abiding people who uphold the Constitution. I support the community and don't break any laws. Hope that's the impression I'm giving you."

"Of course. That's one of the reasons we thought you'd be a good subject for a cover profile. I hope I haven't done anything to make you think differently."

He slid a quick glance at her. "Not so far."

Whatever else he might have said was interrupted by the ringing of his cell phone, resting in a cup holder. Terry tried to see the readout on the screen, but Morgan pulled it up to his ear too fast.

"Yeah. What's up? Uh huh. Uh huh. I can't answer that at the moment. Meet me at my house in fifteen. Yeah. Okay."

He disconnected the call and slid the phone back into the holder.

"Problem?" she asked.

"There always is in a business this size."

"Hope you can at least get some rest."

His laugh held no humor. "Rest seems to be for other people.'

"I'm scheduled to meet with you again tomorrow at nine," she reminded him. "Will that still be on?"

"I'll text you if it changes.

"Of course." What else could she say? And what the hell was the phone call about that set up a meeting this late at night? "See you in the morning."

She made herself stand in front of the doors and wave to him as he drove off. Then she sprinted across the lobby, waited impatiently for an elevator, and raced to her room. The moment she was inside, with the door double locked, she dug out the coded phone Max Jaeger had given her and punched in his two digit number.

"It must be hot if you're calling me this late at night," he greeted her.

"I don't know if it is or not, but somehow we need to find out."

She told him everything she could remember about the evening, including the incidents with Lyle Beckett and her reaction to the man.

"I'm sending you his pictures," she told him. "I've never come across him before so run him through every facial rec program we have. He supposedly owns a hedge fund, which as you know can easily be a conduit for multiple illegal activities. I just get a bad feeling about him."

"I trust those feelings, Terry. We'll check him out ASAP.

"That same feeling tells me this sudden meeting might be with Beckett. I don't like that man."

"This might be one of the breaks we're waiting for," Jaeger pointed out. "See what you can get out of him in the morning."

"Will do. And send me anything you get on Beckett."

She stripped and pulled on a sleep shirt, climbing into bed with the hope she'd be able to get a few hours of shuteye. Instead she tossed and turned, never sleeping more than a few minutes at a time. By morning, her body was exhausted, and she needed a long shower, a pot of coffee, and an expert makeup job to look and feel semi-human.

She got to Morgan's office at quarter to nine, not wanting to be late, especially today. His admin was not at her desk, but his office door was slightly open. She stepped up to it to knock but froze when she heard Lyle Beckett's voice inside.

"I'm telling you, Reed, there's something funny about her." Beckett' voice. "There's something about her that makes my antenna do a jive dance. And Nita Gooding, who may be the bitch of the world but has good instincts, feels the same way."

"Nita feels that way about any female she thinks is going to upstage her. This woman's credentials checked out," Morgan told him. "I spoke with the publisher myself."

"Yeah? Well, who else has she worked for? What other articles has she shown you?"

"Cut it out," Morgan snapped. "She had a portfolio and checked out top to bottom."

"Those things can be faked," Beckett reminded him. "I just get very bad vibes from her. Why take a chance? We can't do that, this close to Zero Hour. You need to get rid of her."

"And how do you propose I do that? You don't think people will pile on if a reporter for *American Arms* just up and disappears? I didn't think you were that stupid."

"Watch who you're calling stupid," Beckett snapped. "You need to find a way. Use that complex brain of yours."

"First of all, I can't just cut the interview short," Morgan protested. "She'll be even more suspicious if I do. I mean, if she is at all," he added. "You're the only one so far who's said anything about it."

"Because I have the best antennae," Beckett pointed out. "And not to damage your fragile ego, but I think this whole magazine profile is a cover for something else."

"Like what? I told you I contacted her publisher and her editor both, and they vouched for her."

"They could have been forced to," Beckett pointed out. "Most people have secrets in their background that put them in vulnerable positions. You used to be more like me, not trusting anyone or anything. What the fuck has happened to you?"

"Nothing." Morgan's voice was harsh. "And I don't need your insults."

"Yeah? You don't think it's strange that this article comes up right when we're planning the biggest event this country has ever seen? Bigger than Oklahoma City? Bigger than 9/11?"

"Believe me, I'm not taking her at face value. I contacted the magazine before I ever agreed to this. I say again, everything checked out. And she hasn't crossed any lines with her questioning."

"Damn, Reed." Beckett's voice had an angry edge to it. "You're usually the one questioning everything."

"I always have my suspicions," Reed pointed out. "But, so far, she's passed every test."

"Then either I'm losing my touch," Beckett told him, "or she's a lot better than I give her credit for. You've got to handle this. Zero Hour is too big and too important to let some female fuck it up. We're already moving men to the ranch and starting the drills. We can't take any chances. Launch day is too close." Pause. "Unless you've changed your mind?"

"Assuming you're right, what do you suggest?"

"First, we need to up the schedule. Get everyone to Montana, sequester them so there's no chance for leaks, and, like I said, start running drills."

"I can't argue with that. What else?"

"Get this woman in a room and find out what the hell is going on, even if you have to beat it out of her."

Terry's stomach clenched. She knew Reed Morgan would have no qualms about torturing her to death to get information. Despite the polite appearance he'd been wearing for her benefit, she knew for a fact he was a ruthless, cold-blooded individual who let nothing step in his way. She had to get out of here, but she wanted to hear the rest of this.

"All right. Then we'll get rid of her."

"Arrange for some kind of accident for this bitch." Beckett's voice was harsh and inflexible. "One that won't look suspicious to the cops. Or to whoever is behind her. You know how to do this. Get her out of this building. Tell her you have something to show her that deals with the phone call you got last night. You said she already acted suspicious of it. Then get to some isolated area and get the job done. And do it yourself. We can't afford any more hands in this than yours and mine."

"All right."

"One more thing," Beckett said.

"What else, for fuck's sake?" Morgan asked.

"I know you don't like much about me except my money. Just don't think you're gonna put a bullet in me like Gooding did to Vanetta. I'm a lot richer and a lot more bulletproof and can do you a lot more damage, dead or alive."

"I wouldn't dream of it." But Morgan's voice had a strange sound to it.

"Good. We need to focus our energy on finding and eliminating that broad."

Terry couldn't listen to any more of the conversation. She had to leave *now*. Her heart was already racing, and she could feel her blood pressure spike. She turned to leave the office and nearly ran into Morgan's admin, Daria, nearly knocking a coffee mug out of her hand.

"Oh!"

"Sorry, sorry."

They spoke simultaneously.

"Not leaving, are you?" Daria asked. "Mr. Morgan has you down for nine o'clock."

Terry shook her head. "Just taking a quick trip to the ladies' room. Be right back."

She raced from the office, feeling Daria's eyes on her, and took the stairs rather than waiting for the elevator. On her previous visits she'd noted the abundance of security cameras everywhere. She couldn't avoid them. The best she could do when she fled Morgan's office was to get the hell out of there before someone grabbed her and get to where she could lose herself in traffic.

In minutes, she was in her rental car and speeding away from Morgan Arms Manufacturing. When she'd put space between her and the manufacturing facility, she stuck her phone in the cupholder and punched the code for Max Jaeger

"Problem," she spit out the moment he answered.

"Okay. Let's have it."

She repeated everything she'd heard.

"You need to come back to D.C. right now," he told her. "We'll put you in protective custody until this is resolved."

"But we still don't know what he has planned," she pointed out. "Not even a sniff. Only that the launching pad, so to speak, is in Montana"

"I'll take it from here," Jaeger insisted. "You work in enough dangerous situations. I don't want you walking around with a big target on your back. Especially not someplace where he's got his own little private army together. Besides, I'm not surprised it was Beckett he was having the conversation with."

"What did you find out?"

"He's quietly funded radical groups before. He's had his own problems with government regulation, which is why he keeps most of his assets offshore. The government is after him right now on a number of issues. He could easily fund whatever Morgan has in mind and do it gladly. And Terry? He's known to make people disappear. This is not good. You need a team there with you."

"A team will stick out like a sore thumb. I'm a trained agent. This isn't my first crisis. You gave me this assignment because you have faith in me to do it. Then let me do it."

"I just don't want you coming home in a body bag. No, I can't let you do it."

"Max, I can find things out," she protested. "If they're moving everyone to Montana, apparently ahead of schedule, something's about to happen. Let me go there and see what I can find out. I have a good friend who's a county sheriff in the Crazy Mountains not far from where Morgan has his spread. He's familiar with the area, he probably knows as much about Morgan as we do, and he can help me. He's been keeping an eye on the man because he said he's had a bad feeling about him since he bought the land."

"Terry…" Max began.

"It's fine. He understands what to do, and I'd place my life in his hands. As a matter of fact, he's a former SEAL. He can help me and protect me if I need that. Max, you put me on this to find out what the hell was going on and I won't quit until I do. Going to Montana may give us our best clue because Morgan sure as hell isn't opening his mouth. And if you send a team out there, no matter what you do, they'll stick out like a sore thumb. We won't get anything, and it may put their lives at risk."

There was silence on the other end of the line.

"I don't like it," Jaeger said at last.

"Listen, I'm going whether you like it or not. I'm doing this. That's all."

"I can't control you when you're out there rogue, you know that. I know that. Are you sure I can't talk you into just coming back here where we can keep you safe and put a plan together? I don't like this."

"I understand. You keep saying that. I'm sorry you have so little faith in my abilities."

"Damn it," he swore. "It's not that. Just do me one favor.

Terry swallowed a sigh. "Let's have it."

"I want the name of this sheriff and his direct number. If you're off the books with just him, I want to talk to him myself. I'm going to find out every-thing about your sheriff friend including the color of his socks. If one thing turns up wrong, you're done, and so is he."

Terry gave it to him. "What else?"

"Report in each day. Call me on my unlisted personal phone You still have the number?"

"I do."

We'll work it from this end. I can't deny the advantage of having someone on the ground, unfet-tered, to scope things out. But once you find out what's going on, I'm sending in a full team. Do not try to take this asshole down yourself or with people whose training may not be up to it."

Terry swallowed a laugh. She could just imagine Alex Rossi's reaction to that comment.

"Max, I told you. He's a former SEAL. The men on his staff are all former SEALs."

Although she wasn't sure how many he actually had right now.

"Just to repeat, in case you missed it, if one thing turns up wrong, you're done and so is he. Bad enough you're going rogue on me. I can't have some unknown fucking things up."

"That it?"

"No. You'll need a car. It's a long drive, but I don't want to take the chance of you flying out there. Morgan has eyes and ears all over the country, and there are too many chances at airports for him to spot you. It's highly likely a man with his resources and outlook could even have someone hack into airlines databases. Then all he has to do is send someone your picture and you could be dead meat."

"I can handle the drive," she assured him.

"Second. You check in by phone twice a day. That's an order. And keep that phone with you at all times. We'll be digging for information from this end, and we need to keep each other informed."

"Got it. Oh, by the way, I had to leave all my stuff in the room. I wasn't sure if they'd try to find me there. I've got my purse and all my electronics, but that's it. I need to make a stop at a big box store to replenish."

"I'll take care of everything in your room. And I'll

arrange to get cash to you. Hold on." He was back in seconds. "You on Interstate 10?"

"Headed there." And fast, she told herself, because sure as hell someone would be on her tail any second now.

"Okay. Once you're on it, stay on IH-10 East and take the IH-35 Interchange. Call me when you're on IH-35 and you're sure you've lost them. I'll work on getting a clean vehicle for you and let you know where to pick it up."

The connection went dead.

Oh well. Max Jaeger was a great boss but not much of a one for niceties. Of course, in their business there wasn't necessarily time for them. She cranked the engine on her car and headed to the interstate again, still a little shaken from the conversation she'd overheard. She hadn't drawn a full breath since she'd pulled out of the parking lot. She needed a strong coffee to go to make a call on her burner phone.

But then she looked in her rearview mirror and realized they'd both have to wait. A brown SUV was coming up in her rearview mirror. Good thing the interstate entrance was seconds away.

CHAPTER 4

THREE YEARS and he hadn't been able to outrun his demons.

Thirty-six months.

One thousand and ninety-five days.

He couldn't even count the number of miles he'd covered in all that time. But no matter how far he went and how fast, he couldn't seem to outrun the devils perched on his shoulder.

Once he thought he'd found the answer. But then he discovered that to benefit from another person you had to relate to them. That a relationship was give and take, and he seemed to be all about take. Even when he thought he'd found temporary comfort, the eruption of the nightmares chased anyone away.

Work of any kind had been sporadic, mostly because he wasn't sure when an episode would grab him and render him less efficient. Construction seemed to be the best solution. Hammering nails helped to drive away flashbacks and allowed him to vent his anger and distress. At night he could fall into bed exhausted and hope he'd worn himself out too much for the dreams to come back.

What he really wanted was someplace in the wide open spaces. He'd grown up on a ranch in Colorado where his father had been the foreman, but he hadn't tried to go back to it. The fear of an episode grabbing him in the middle of working with horses or cattle or other people kept him away from it. He'd heard about a ranch that specialized in working with people who had PTSD, but he'd had enough of people trying to pick his brain apart. What bothered him the most was that he, the quintessential big bad SEAL, who had been a solid member of his team, had lost his shit and couldn't find it.

He'd had a brief period right after his separation when he thought he was creating a new life for himself. That was when he met Terry with the silky brown hair, the mouthwatering curves, the ocean-blue eyes, and the great sense of humor. Not to mention the off-the-charts sex they couldn't seem to get enough of. For two weeks—a very intense two weeks—he thought he'd actually found someone. But then the nightmares came back and he knew he had to get the hell out of there while he still had some dignity left.

And that was when everything went to shit. The nightmares came back full force. The anger. The resentment. The self-deprecation. And most of all the pain that attacked both his brain and his heart. Oh, he'd wanted to make this work, more than anything, but he wasn't about to inflict himself on a woman like Terry Fordice. She deserved much more than he could give her. So, he'd packed up his crap, left her a note, and taken off to figure out how to handle his life.

He couldn't count the times he thought about her, or the nights he dreamed about her. Or the cold showers he took so his hard-as-concrete dick didn't hit something and break off. For three years he'd done his best to forget her, an impossible task. Maybe, if he could figure out how to do it without destroying himself, it was time to get some help and see if by some slim chance she'd let him back into her life.

Maybe.

Maybe it was time to get his fucking act together.

Two days ago he'd finished his most recent construction job and needed a change of scenery. Maybe that would help. Although it hadn't before. He was about to check out of the No Name Motel in Anytown, USA and jump on his motorcycle when his cell phone rang. He looked at the screen and didn't recognize the number so was tempted to ignore it.

Then he thought, What the hell, and punched the Accept button.

"Yeah?"

"You still lying around some fleabag hotel with your head up your ass?"

The voice took him back to his SEAL team and, for a moment, Jesse was startled. What the fuck? Zane Halstead? No. Impossible. Someone was pranking him.

"Cat got your tongue, Waterboy?"

Damn! It really was Zane. He was the one who'd given Jesse that nickname after a particular mission. When Jesse left the teams, Zane hadn't shown an interest in getting out. But he kept his ear to the ground, and scuttlebutt had it the self-isolated warrior had gone through hell with his injuries and loss of identity when injuries forced him out. Jesse was long gone by then but through the grapevine he learned the hell the guy had gone through.

The man on the other end of the conversation, however, sounded a far cry from what he, Jesse, had been told.

"Uh, just kind of shocked to hear from you after all this time."

Just the thought of it sent a sour taste surging through Jesse's mouth. Why had he ever thought he'd love civilian life? But he'd been burned out and needed to leave before he made a mistake that endangered someone else.

There was a slight pause.

"I probably would be if some asshole hadn't shot me up and damaged my shoulder and hip."

"Well, damn!" Jesse knew that, just from scuttlebutt he'd picked up here and there, and could feel the man's pain. "So how long you been out?"

"Almost eighteen months now, and you wouldn't believe how good my life is now. After a rocky start, I might add."

Jesse was glad for the man, but he hated that green wave of jealousy that raced through him.

"That right? Doing what?"

"Well, see, that's kind of what I called about." Another pause. "I been tracking down SEALs I knew who aren't active duty any longer and telling them about this."

Jesse shifted on the bed, leaning back against the headboard. He figured he might as well get comfortable because Zane didn't seem to be in any hurry to hang up. And he wanted to know exactly what *this* was.

"Okay, let's have it."

"You aren't hooked up with anything at the moment, right?"

Jesse grunted. "If you went to all the trouble of tracking me down, then you already know that. How the hell did you find me, anyway?"

Zane laughed. "I've got someone who could find the Invisible Man, and he's doing a good job of it. I figured you might be through wandering the world and interesting in trying something that utilized your special skills. He's got just the setup for that but without all that stress."

"And just who is this talented person?"

"His name is Alex Rossi." One second of silence. "Sheriff Alex Rossi. In Montana. In the Crazy Mountains."

"Yeah? And what makes him so good?"

"For one thing," Zane answered, "he's a former SEAL. That ought to be enough to spark your interest"

"Hooyah." But he uttered the battle cry in a skeptical tone.

"I'm not blowing smoke here, Waterboy. The former sheriff here went to prison, and Rossi was hired to take over and clean up the mess. A job that required a lot of skills, including toughness and dedication. Long story, which I'll tell you when I see you, because I *do* plan on that happening."

Jesse shifted on the bed. "Okay, what's the situation now that prompted this phone call.? Out of the blue, I might add."

"I'd say we might have gotten together sooner if I'd known where you were keeping your ass," Zane pointed out. "But one of my extracurricular activities is helping Alex track down former SEALs who would be an asset to this sheriff's office."

"And just why is he doing that?"

"I told you, he's cleaning house here," Zane reminded him. "He's only kept one former deputy. A woman, by the way, who can easily put the rest of us to shame. He wants to replace everyone else with former SEALs." He paused. "That's his goal."

Jesse frowned at something he sensed in the tone of Zane's voice.

"What about that aren't you telling me?"

Silence.

"Jesse?" he prodded.

"Give it up."

"Okay, but look at this as a positive thing. Alex had some, uh, challenges when he left the SEALs. He got his act together and became a top-notch lawman. Now he wants to hire those of us who also had challenges to deal with assimilating back into civilian life, either from physical or psychological situations. I was skeptical as hell when he first contacted me, but so far it's working very well." The sound of his throat clearing bubbled over the connection. "I think this could be just what you need, Jesse."

Jesse gripped the cell phone so hard he almost cracked the case.

"So, someone told this Alex that I'm looney tunes and need a place to get my act together?"

"Jesus, Jesse." Zane barked a short laugh. "No. It means I spoke to Rossi and made him aware of your skills. He wants you to come talk to him. Check it out for yourself. And if it works, it can benefit both you and the sheriff."

"What exactly is he doing with a bunch of misfits, and what do you want of me?"

"Hey." Zane gave a short laugh. "Watch it with the misfits stuff. Some of us may have a lot of adjusting to do, but our skills are still top drawer."

"Okay, okay, okay. So, what's the deal?"

"Alex—Sheriff Rossi—asked me to help him find people who would be good candidates for deputy slots. I knew you'd left the Teams, thought maybe you were managing to get your shit together, and passed along your name. He'd like you to come out here, meet him, check out the setup, and see if you think you 'd like to give this a shot."

Jesse wasn't sure what to say. This was an avenue he hadn't even thought of, although he knew a lot of SEALs as well as other Special Forces guys had gone into security. He didn't know how many had actually picked law enforcement for the next stage of their lives. Should he do this? Take a chance? He could always say no, right?

"I just don't want him to look at me as some psychological mess because I'm not."

Zane's laugh echoed across the connection.

"Believe me, if that's what he sees after he meets you, you'll be gone before you know what hit you." There was the sound of him clearing his throat again. "My challenges were physical, but I got past that, and

Alex never treated me any differently. What do you say?"

Well, what else did he have to do, anyway? Maybe this time the situation would help him get Terry Fordice out of his mind.

"Okay. I'll give it a shot. But," he added quickly, "this is just a looksee. No promises."

"On either side," Zane agreed.

"Text me the directions. I've got your number in my phone now, so I'll let you know when I get close." When he read the information, he said, "I'm less than a day away."

"Call me when you're partway here, just to check in."

Jesse laughed. "Think I'll change my mind?".

"Better not. You might be missing out on something great."

Jesse wasn't so sure about that, but he kicked back on the bed for long moments after the call ended. What did he really have to lose, anyway? He'd already planned to find someplace new where construction was hiring and see if that might be a place to get his head on straight. Yeah, his head. That seemed to be fucked up, especially when he tried to clear it of thoughts about Terry Fordice.

Swallowing a sigh, he rose and stuffed everything in the small duffel that fit in one compartment of his bike. Ten minutes later he had checked out, picked up breakfast at a drive through, and was on the road to

Montana. To the Crazy Mountains. Yeah, that was very appropriate, because he had to be crazy to do this.

The roads he took were mostly rural. He avoided the major highways whenever possible, preferring to enjoy the scenery rather than breathe the exhaust from all the cars. For some reason, today the trip made him think of Terry Fordice again. He'd bought the beast just before they met, and he'd taken her riding on it a bunch. Now his horny mind thought back to the times he'd convinced her to ride in front of him, her perfect ass pressed against his fly and the swollen cock behind it. God, that woman was hot. Best sex of his life, and she was smart, sassy, and funny on top of it.

Well, he'd sure fucked that up in a hurry. His mind and his nightmares had betrayed him, leading him to decide he couldn't handle a relationship. Not the first mistake he'd made nor the last one. Since then any woman he took to bed had turned out to be a pale comparison. His cock—and shockingly, his brain—had been giving him hell since then. He needed to do his best to get her out of his mind, since the chances of ever seeing her again were slim to none.

When he stopped to gas up the Harley Davidson Ultra Glide he checked the remaining distance on his digital map and called Zane.

"Well, I'm halfway there," he told the man. "I guess

I'll finish the trip. I'd hate for you to get all pissed off at me."

Zane laughed. "You know I would. Okay, get your sorry butt back on the road. You should be here before dark. Call me again when you're very close, and I'll tell you how to get where I am. Even with GPS, places in the Crazy Mountains aren't that easy to find."

"Will do."

He climbed back on the bike and kicked on the motor. He hoped to hell he wasn't making the biggest mistake of his life.

TERRY THOUGHT it was a good thing she'd had a course in evasive driving. She was barely hauling ass down the road leading away from Morgan Arms Manufacturing when she saw a brown SUV barreling up behind her. Flooring the accelerator—and giving thanks for her course in evasive driving—she hit the interstate and zoomed across three lanes of traffic. The SUV was still on her tail but caught behind a semi and an oil truck, unable to cross the lanes. While they were still blocked, she pushed her speed past the limit, zigzagging back and forth until she came close to the intersection with IH-35. Waiting until the last possible minute, she zipped across the lanes again and took the exit ramp to the other highway.

She didn't let out her breath until she was five minutes onto the other interstate and could see nothing of the SUV. Sliding into the flow of traffic, she pressed a speed dial number on her cell and called Alex Rossi, a Montana sheriff who was her good friend. If anyone could help her, he was it.

He listened to her story and, as he usually did, asked a few pointed questions before agreeing with her that he could help.

"Check in along the way," he told her. "We'll handle it, Terry. I'd love to tie a rope around that asshole. I always believed there was something wrong about him."

"Well, now you know. And thanks for agreeing to help me. See you sometime tomorrow."

"I'll start putting things together. Drive safe."

She got off at an exit that would take her to a large mall, zigzagged around it, and finally managed to find a parking space between two pickups. Just as she pulled in her phone rang. She looked at the read-out. Jaeger.

"I'm still alive," she told him as soon as he answered.

"Good. That's what I like to hear. Where are you?"

She told him her location, giving him the name of the mall where she was parked so he could pinpoint her on a map.

"Okay, don't stay parked, just in case. Drive around the parking lot to make sure those assholes haven't by some miracle located you. Give it a good twenty minutes. I'm going to text you a location. When you get there, a man named Brian will be waiting for you with a clean car and driving directions to where you're going. Brian will let me know when you're on your way again. Stop wherever you need to get supplies, but don't try to make it in one day. I know you."

Yes, he did. If the situation hadn't been so dire, she'd have laughed.

"Got it."

"Check in again when you make your first stop."

The line went dead. That was Max. Efficient as hell with no time for niceties. It didn't matter to her. He had her back, and that was all she cared about.

Twenty minutes later she pulled off the interstate and into a used car lot. When she stopped at the trailer that served as the office, a tall, lean man with graying hair and a trimmed beard was waiting by the steps. She left the car running and her gun tucked against her thigh where she'd kept it since leaving Morgan Arms. She wasn't taking any chances.

The man walked up to the car and nodded. "I'm Brian. I've got your car."

Could she believe it was him and not an imposter?

Get real, Terry. Reed Morgan and Lyle Beckett have no

idea where you are and would not have had time to set this whole thing up.

But then, as if aware of what she was thinking, he said, "His middle name is Howard."

Terry swallowed a laugh. Max hated that name. Only someone he knew and trusted would have it.

"Okay." She shut off the car and stepped out, taking her purse and her weapon.

"Max said you're heading to Montana, to the Crazies. Got you a sturdy ride." He led her to the side of the trailer where a black SUV sat waiting.

Terry almost laughed. SUVs seemed to be taking over her life.

"Thank you." She accepted the keys he handed her and listened while he ran over the details of the vehicle for her. Then he handed her an envelope.

"Cash," he told her. "Max said you needed it."

"Right." No credit cards for her right now. "Thanks."

"Crank up that car and let me go over a few things with you."

Ten minutes later she was back on IH-35 with directions to Bozeman, Montana programmed into her phone and a wad of cash in her purse. She planned to put plenty of miles between her and San Antonio before she stopped to pick up what she needed and get her cup of well-deserved coffee.

CHAPTER 5

"WHAT DO YOU MEAN, you lost her?" Reed Morgan stared at the two men standing in front of his desk. "You guys are supposed to be the best. She's just a fucking reporter, for god's sake."

Lyle Beckett sat in a casual pose with one hip on a corner of the desk, but the line of his body was anything but, and anger radiated from his body.

"Just what I said." Curt Renshaw, his personal bodyguard, spoke in a rigid tone. "We lost her on the interstate. I don't think I've ever seen a reporter drive the way she does."

"Told you," Beckett snapped. "If she's a reporter, I'm Little Bo Peep."

Morgan maintained his rigid control with an effort. He was damn fucking sick of Beckett throwing his weight around. Sure, it had been a godsend when he stepped up into the financial hole left when they'd had to get rid of Vanetti. Now, however, he wondered if it was worth the cost. The man challenged his authority at every turn.

He focused on Renshaw again, shocked at the situation. Renshaw never lost a target, never misplaced anyone, never let a situation slip away. He could tell the man was angry with himself and trying to control it.

"Give me the details. You got to her before she pulled out of the parking area, right?"

"Maybe a couple of minutes after, but we were right on her tail. Maybe not more than three car lengths behind her when we hit the interstate."

"So, what happened?" Morgan demanded.

"The minute she hit IH-10 she took off like she had a stick of dynamite up her ass."

Don, the other man, agreed. "She rode that interstate traffic like a pro. When we got up to the 35 interchange, she zipped across three lanes of traffic and onto 35. No way we could follow her."

"I never met a damn reporter who could drive like that," Renshaw spat. "She's a phony, whatever else she is. I should have spotted that from the beginning, but the bitch is a damn good actor."

Morgan wanted to hit someone or something at the look Beckett shot his way.

"So, what you're saying is she took off on IH-35 West, and you lost her."

"By the time we were able to get off one highway

and onto the other," Emery told him, "she was in the wind."

Morgan wanted to hit something. Or some*one*. How the hell did he get a ringer in here, anyway? He'd called Franklin Morrow, the publisher of *American Made* himself to check her out. Why would Morrow lie to him? Did someone have his balls in a wringer?

Fuck, fuck, fuck.

"What do you want us to do?" Renshaw asked. "Let me loose on this. I'll find her."

"No. Do nothing right now. I have to figure this out. There's a good possibility she's with the fucking government. I don't want you tripping any warning flags. Just keep yourself available." He looked at Emery. "Both of you."

He could tell that Renshaw was keeping himself under tight control. If Beckett had not been in the room, he might have protested. Instead he just gave silent agreement and the two men left.

Beckett slid off the corner of the desk, standing so he faced Morgan. "It is critical that we find this bitch."

Morgan held up a hand. He was getting sick of Beckett's criticism and increasing attempts at control. Project Zero Hour was going to be expensive. They'd had to make a lot of plans and arrange for a lot of equipment to pull this off. Vanetti's unexpected defection had put him in a bind, and Beckett had seemed like a godsend.

Yeah. God of the underworld.

But he was right about this. Had he let his ego get in the way here? His whole life he'd had a laser focus on his goals. He couldn't believe he'd missed so badly on this one.

"You're right." He pulled up his list of contacts on his cell phone. "Everyone has footprints somewhere. Plus, we've got a network that covers the country. We need to put it to use for this. We'll find her."

TERRY LIFTED the cup from the holder in the console and took a last swallow of the now cold coffee. She'd be damned glad to get to Eagle Rock and Alex Rossi after all this time on the road. She'd spent last night in Colorado in a cheap but clean roadside motel before hitting IH 25 again toward Billings. The SUV was built for long distance travel with comfortable seats and a lot of electronics. She'd just be glad to get to Alex's office and off the road for a while.

She had left the interstate a while ago and was enjoying the scenery as she followed the two-lane highway that would lead her to Alex Rossi's office. Alex had been on the same SEAL team as her cousin Rick. Sadly, Rick had been killed by an IED, and Alex had come to visit her aunt and uncle and talk to them about Rick's time on the team. There had been no romantic spark between them, but they had become good friends and kept in touch sporadically. She was glad he'd found a woman like Micki Schroeder and that they were happy together. And thrilled he'd not only made a place for himself in the civilian world using the skills he'd been trained in, but also that he was reaching out to other SEALs to do the same thing.

When she'd called him about the situation with Reed Morgan, he'd told her to come on out, no questions asked, and let him know what he could do to help.

She had spoken to Max Jaeger three times since she'd left Texas yesterday, aware he'd managed to get eyes on Reed Morgan shortly after her hasty exit.

"He's been holed up in his office since you left," Max told her. "We've got a fake construction crew working on the access road, so we'll know as soon as he leaves. I also flagged his license plate so when he drives anywhere that has CCTV we can follow him."

"The man whose picture I sent you, Lyle Beckett. Anything on him?"

"Not as much as we'd like, but enough to know he's got money to burn and suddenly became asshole buddies with Morgan. With Vanetti dead, Morgan needed a new money man. He's rich, but he's building up to something we think requires unlimited cash. The worrisome thing is that Beckett, like

Morgan, has a grudge against the government. What-ever Morgan has on his agenda, it appears Beckett is more than willing to fund it. Which, if I may say so, scares the shit out of me."

"You'll keep looking into it?"

"Count on it."

They had spoken briefly when she checked into the motel last night and then this morning after she hit the highway. She was just anxious to get there and look around. Alex had told her Morgan's property, while private, was connected to the huge ranch next to it. And that ranch was owned by a friend of Alex's, which could give them the access they needed to Morgan's spread. She was anxious to get a look at the setup and fix it in her mind. Try to figure out what the hell they were doing there, before Morgan pulled the trigger on whatever he was planning.

In Colorado, before she'd gone to sleep for the night, she'd hit a discount store and used some of the money Max had arranged for her to buy some basic clothing and other needs. At least she was set for the time being.

She paid careful attention to the scenery as she ate up the highway miles. All around her she could see the peaks of the Crazy Mountains rising, where the transition from prairie to mountain was incred-ibly dramatic. She knew most of the land surrounding it was privately held. Landowners were obsessive about keeping traffic to an absolute minimum. There were, however, two public access roads, one from the east and the other from the west. She hoped using one of them would get her close enough to Reed Morgan's spread to find out what the hell was going on.

It was late afternoon, and she was less than a mile from Alex's office when disaster hit. The sound of a blown tire and the *clump* on the road let her know exactly what had happened. Pulling over to the shoulder, she turned off the ignition and climbed out, the view of the left rear tire confirming what she thought. Flat tire.

"Well, damn."

Not at all what she needed. She'd changed plenty of flats in her time, but it was a pain in the ass, and she really wasn't in the mood.

"Well, better get to it, girl. No white knight is going to come along and save you."

She supposed she could call Alex, as close as she was, but her streak of independence wouldn't let her do it. Instead, with a sigh, she climbed out of the vehicle. She had the jack lying next to the flat and had just pulled the spare out of the well where it was stored when she heard the sound of a motorcycle behind her. She grabbed her gun from her purse next to the driver's seat and shoved it into the pocket of the new jeans she wore, pulling her T-shirt out of the waistband and letting it hang loose to disguise the outline of the weapon.

As the motorcycle came closer, her breath caught. No, it couldn't be. Not here, in the middle of nowhere. Not when her mind was so focused on her job and what her immediate priority was. It had to be someone who just reminded her of him, with a big bike that looked like his. But when he got closer, every nerve in her body fired as she realized it was indeed Jesse Donovan, heading straight for her. What on earth was he doing here?

He pulled up to the shoulder of the road, shut off his engine, and climbed off the bike. Then he pulled off his helmet and stared at her for a long moment. She felt as if all her clothes had been stripped off.

"Fancy meeting you here," he said at last. His voice still had that deep, rusty tone to it.

She ran her gaze over his body. He was just as lean and muscular, his hair a little longer, his beard a little scruffier. Very inappropriately, the pulse between her legs set up a throbbing, and her nipples hardened. She wished she had a jacket on to conceal the evidence of her unwanted arousal because Jesse's eyes immediately focused on her breasts.

She swallowed. "I could say the same."

"I'm here to see an old friend. What's your story?"

"Ditto." He knew she was an ATFE agent, but she wasn't about to give him any details of what was going on. She had no reason not to trust him, but spilling her guts didn't go with the job.

"You have an old friend out here in the middle of the Crazy Mountains? That's...crazy!"

"Yeah, well, I could say the same." She looked at her flat and the jack lying on its side. "I'd better get to work here."

Jesse closed his fingers around her wrists, his touch sending arrows of heat through her body.

"I'll do it." He grinned. "Wouldn't want you to break a fingernail."

"Damn you, Jesse."

She wanted to stamp her foot at the unfortunate situation. Then she wanted to scream.

He laughed. "You wouldn't be the first person to say that. Now, let me at it. I'll get this done in just a minute."

Silence dropped over them, and she felt a need to break it.

"So, uh, what have you been doing since I last saw you?"

His body tensed for a moment before he answered. "A little of this, a little of that. Here and there. Lot of construction work."

"Oh."

She wanted to ask him if he'd hooked up with anyone, but pride kept her from it.

"You still chasing the bad guys?" he asked.

"Still doing it. They never stop being bad."

It seemed they had nothing to say to each other after that, so she just stood and watched him.

He changed the tire and, as he was tightening the lug nuts, he asked, "So, who are you all the way out here to see, anyway? Old boyfriend?"

"I'm here on business."

"Here in the Crazies?"

"Good place for crazy people," she told him.

"And who are you on your way to meet? Another hotshot ATFE agent?"

"Not that it's any of your business," she snapped, "but I'm hooking up with a friend who's going to help me."

"And does this friend have a name?" He finished tightening the last lug nut.

"You wouldn't know him. Alex Rossi. Sheriff Alex Rossi."

Jesse dropped the lug wrench with a clang and whirled to look at her.

"You have got to be kidding me."

"Why? He's an old friend. And what's it to you, anyway?"

He raked his fingers through his hair. "That's who I'm on my way to meet with. He's an old friend of mine from the SEALs. We were on the same team for a while, as a matter of fact."

Terry just stared at him. "You're kidding me. Or someone is playing a huge joke."

"Nope. Not at all." He rose, replaced the lug wrench in rear well of her SUV along with the flat and dusted his hands on his jeans. "But it is a hell of a coincidence."

"No kidding."

Silence dropped between them like a boulder.

"Listen, Terry," he began

"Jesse, I—" She stopped, took a deep breath. What could she say to him that didn't sound like a bitchy female? He was certainly free to do whatever he wanted, including leaving her without a word.

He held up a hand. "Me first. Running out on you the way I did was wrong. I knew it then, and I still know it, but I didn't know what else to do."

"All you had to do was tell me we were getting too serious and you wanted to back off. Or needed to get out. Anything but just running off."

He nodded, an anxious look in his eyes. "I was carrying a lot of baggage. A lot. Stuff I couldn't make myself discuss." Distress etched lines in his face. "I still can't, and it isn't fair to dump that on another person."

She wanted to tell him she could handle anything he dished out, but she knew at the moment he wasn't open to that. Maybe this coincidental meeting was fate creating the opportunity. She mentally crossed her fingers because Jesse Donovan was the only man she'd ever been with where she could just plain be herself.

"I'll tell you what. Let's get to Alex's office and let

him know we're both here. After that, who knows?"
She shrugged.

"I know you have a job to do, but I'm sure we'll be
thrown together. I don't want you to be uncomfortable with me."

"I'm a big girl. I can handle it. And thanks for
changing the tire." She forced a smile. "Since I know
where Alex's office is, how about following me so we
can get going?"

He studied her for a long moment, something
swirling in his eyes that she couldn't identify. Then
he nodded. "Let's do it."

Terry cranked her ignition and pulled onto the
highway, waited until Jesse had his motorcycle
revved, and took off down the road. Her emotions
were chasing each other all over the place, and she
needed to pull them in. She had to focus on Reed
Morgan and whatever he might be planning. That
was the most important thing. Jesse Donovan could
do his thing with Alex—whatever that might be—but
she wanted first call on the sheriff's time. Reed
Morgan and whatever he was up to was more important than anything Jesse could possibly have in mind.

It seemed like only seconds before she turned off
the two-lane highway and onto a short gravel road
that led to the parking area where the building was
located. Three SUVs with the logo of the sheriff's
office were parked there along with a pickup and two
sedans. Sliding her SUV into a slot at the edge of the

parking area, she waited for Jesse to dismount from his bike and hang his helmet on the handlebars.

He looked around.

"It's pretty much out here by itself, isn't it?"

"Most of the county is privately owned land

"After you." His mouth curved in a hint of a grin. "Ladies first."

The building itself was one story, painted tan, with a porch that ran across the front. Next to the double doors leading to the interior was a neat plaque proclaiming it the office of the sheriff. Terry climbed the three stairs and pushed through the doors. She smiled at the woman sitting at a desk behind a window. Angela Pascal had been Alex's admin since he took over the office. Terry had met her on a brief stopover two years earlier.

She grinned at the woman. "Hey, Angela."

"Nice to see you, Miss Fordice."

"I told you to call me Terry, remember?" she reminded the woman. "Is he in?"

"Yes, and he's right here."

Terry turned to the tall man wearing knife-creased pants that covered the longest legs she'd ever seen. A holstered gun rode one lean hip. He embraced her with a genuine hug.

"Good to see you, Terry." He winked. "Even if you did bring what might be a shitload of trouble with you."

She laughed. "Good to see you, too."

Alex looked over her shoulder. "And you must be Jesse Donovan. I didn't know you two knew each other. Did you come here together?"

The two men shook hands.

"Uh, yeah, we know each other and, no, we didn't travel here together. We sort of ran into each other on the road."

"Coincidence," Terry added. "I had a flat, and Jesse stopped to change it for me. Lucky for me we were both headed here and that he happened along right when I could use an extra set of hands."

Alex looked back at Jesse. "Glad you decided to take Zane up on his invitation. He'd planned to be here after he got your call, but he's out chasing some idiot shooting at cattle."

"No problem."

Terry glanced at Jesse and realized he looked a little uncomfortable. She desperately needed to sit down with Alex and find out what he'd learned and what he had in place, but she wasn't sure how much she should tell Jesse. Maybe she should let him go in first.

"If you guys want to meet first, go ahead." She did her best to tamp down her impatience.

Alex looked from her to Jesse and back again. "Actually, Terry, if you have no objections, I'd like to have Jesse sit in with us. He might be a help in this situation, and it would give him a chance to see what's what here."

"Uh, sure." And thanks for putting me in an awkward position.

"You said you know each other. If there's a problem here, let's have it. It can affect both circumstances."

Did she know Jesse enough to trust him with a hush-hush operation? He'd certainly never given her reason to doubt him when they'd been together—until he left without a word. But that was personal. And he was a SEAL. While no outfit was perfect, for the most part SEALs had an unblemished reputation. Alex himself was a prime example of that. And she'd realized on the long drive here that she really might need help if she was going to find out exactly what Reed Morgan was up to.

"No." She shook her head. "No problem."

"Good." Alex nodded. "You said this was urgent, so let's get to it, but I don't want to do it here in this office. I trust most of the people who walk in and out, but I can't always control the traffic."

"Is there a place to stay around here?" Jesse asked. "Maybe we can meet there."

"No place with privacy, but I have something to suggest to both of you. Zane and Lainie have the house I lived in when I first got here." He grinned. "Now I get to live in the big house with the head of the ranch." Then his smile disappeared. "But only for what I hope is a short while. We're hoping someone buys the damn place soon and we can build on ten acre we're keeping for ourselves."

No one said anything for a moment. Terry knew all about Alex's marriage to Micki Schroeder, whose family owned one of the huge ranches at the foothills of the Crazies. One of his first cases was to solve the murder of Micki's father who turned out to be part of a group of uber wealthy ranchers that thought it was fun to rape and threaten underage girls and kill them if they talked. They were protected by the previous sheriff who was now in jail himself. Schroeder's only saving grace was his intention to come clean, which is what had gotten him killed.

Alex had helped Micki through the devastating time. Now they were married and anxious to put the past behind them. They were building a new life now just as Alex was rebuilding the sheriff's office.

"Anyway," Alex went on, "the point of the conversation is, there is a place with privacy. There were a couple of other houses like the one Zane and Lainie have that were for sale. Micki and I bought them to have available for SEALs I invited to join my staff. If they accept, they get a place to live in rent free for a year. If they stay past that, they either buy the house, pay rent, or find a different place to live."

Jesse cocked an eyebrow. "And how's that working out for you?"

Alex laughed. "I'll let you know. You're only the

second one I've invited. Zane gave you a high recommendation."

"Yeah, I can imagine," Jesse muttered, and shook
his head.

Terry drew her eyebrows together in a frown.
"But that means you still have a very small staff."

"True. Miranda Golden and Zane are it at the
moment for full-timers. I did, on Miranda's recommendation, hire two part-time deputies who said
they're good until I fill all the spots. Jesse, if you try
this out and decide you want to stay, there's definitely a slot for you."

"This is a damn big county to police," Jesse
pointed out.

"It is. Fortunately, except for that one fucking
mess, not much happens here. If it does I can call on
the state police to help. In any event, think you two
could share one of those houses? They're big enough
you won't trip over each other unless you want to.
And Micki sent a cleaning crew in to get it ready."

Terry looked at Jesse, whose eyes were filled with
such a swirl of emotions she didn't know what to say.
He'd walked away from her before. Would he share a
house with her?"

"I can always—" she began.

"We'll do it," Jesse said at the same time.

Great. She was going to be staying in the same
house with the man who'd dumped her like yesterday's trash yet still made very pulse point in her body

pound in response to his presence, not to mention her traitorous nipples that hardened to almost painful points.

Her pulse thumped a little harder, and her mouth went dry. It would take a lot of discipline to stay focused with Jesse Donovan in such close proximity. How the hell was she going to do this?

Alex leaned back and smiled. "Glad that's settled. Jesse, you'll get a chance to see what we do here and how we do it so you can decide if you want to give it a shot."

"Sounds like a plan. Got directions?"

"You both can just follow me. Let me tell Angela we're leaving. Oh, and I'll want her to send Zane over when he gets back." He looked at Terry. "If I have to, I'll read Miranda in on this. You can trust her 100 percent, and we may need her before this is over. She knows this area like the back of her hand. If there's some reason Morgan is using his place as a staging area, she'll be the one to tell you. Okay, let's move."

Alex led them out to the front are and stopped to speak to the receptionist.

"Angela, I'll be out for a while at the house near the Halsteads. I'll have my phone with me, but don't put anything through unless it's a national emergency. The only exception is Zane, if he gets here. You can tell him where we are and send him along. Jesse? I guess we'll find out real quick what you're made of and if this here interests you."

"Uh, okay." Terry wasn't all that happy about increasing their little group, but she trusted Alex, so that had to be enough for her.

Five minutes later, a stew of emotions swirling around inside her, she was following Alex down the two-lane country road, Zane behind her, and Jesse bringing up the rear. For the first time in a long time, she felt uncertain, and about more than Reed Morgan.

CHAPTER 6

THE FIRST THING Terry did when she got back in her car, ready to follow Alex to the house where she'd be staying, was call Max and tell him about Jesse Donovan.

"Isn't he—"

"Yes," she snapped, cutting off the rest of his question. "He is. You ran a check on him then, if you recall because god forbid my private life should be private."

"You're in a business where nothing is private," he reminded her. "Too many people want to breach our security."

"I know, I know. Let's just move on., He came up clean that time, and I'm sure nothing has changed."

"But you'll run him again, anyway," Jaeger pointed out."

"Fine. Just let me know the result as soon as you

94

can. I'm about to sit down with him and Alex Rossi If there's a problem, which I do not expect, I need to know now."

"Is there another way? I'll be back to you in no more than thirty."

"Max?"

"Yeah?"

"Uh. Thanks for not cutting the lifeline completely."

He chuffed a short laugh. "Terry, you may be determined to go rogue on this, but you're one of my top agents. I don't want anything to happen to you if I can help it."

Terry often wondered how Max got answers to some of his questions so quickly. Then she realized that to hold the position he did, there had to be absolute trust and confidence from the higher ups.

Fifteen minutes later they were all at the house Alex had led them to. The first thing Terry did was find the coffee machine—thank the lord it was a single serving type—and fix a cup of coffee for herself. The others followed suit and then they were ready to get down to business. As far as Terry was concerned, it couldn't happen too fast for her. They had just seated themselves around the dining room table when her phone beeped with a message.

"You're on your own because the boss wants to work it from here, so please don't get yourself killed. Check in on my other phone when you call. Max."

Okay, then. Time to get down to business.

She was never more grateful for her hard-won discipline than she was sitting in the meeting with Alex and Jesse. It allowed her to focus on what could be a national emergency and bottle up her reaction to Jesse Donovan. She'd been fighting it since he pulled up behind her on the highway and all those ruthlessly depressed hormones screamed and jumped to be let loose.

But she was a professional, and her work came first, so she ruthlessly closed her mind to the effect the man had on her and concentrated on the task at hand. In careful, concise sentences, she laid out the situation, explaining that the government believed Reed Morgan was planning some act against the government that would be both dangerous and destructive. She gave them the background information she had on both Morgan and Beckett plus the confirmed knowledge that the ranch was the gathering place as well as the launching pad for whatever was about to happen.

"Whatever it is," she finished, "it's going to make a big splash."

For a long moment Alex said nothing, just sat there as if absorbing her information. Then he looked at Jesse.

"Zane said you were part of a SEAL team that took down a terrorist group in Afghanistan. One that was planning to blow up a critical base."

"That's right." Jesse looked away for a moment. "I was also part of the team that managed to nail down the information in the first place."

"Whatever this guy is plotting, this could be right up your alley." His mouth curved in a half-grin. "Talk about the right person at the right time."

"Do you know Reed Morgan?" Terry asked. "Have you met him?"

"Once. He has about two hundred acres not far from my office here. Tight-assed and tight-lipped. Have no idea what he does there since he doesn't run any cattle. He also doesn't socialize with anyone in this county or the next. The ranchers here, although separated by thousands of acres of land, are a pretty tight group. That's why it took me so long to break the case that brought me here."

Jesse leaned forward. "What was that about?"

Alex shook his head. "That's for another time. My point is, Morgan's made himself an unknown factor. We've got to find a way to see what's being put together."

"Which is why I came to you," Terry told him. "You know this place like the back of your hand. You can give me the geography of the place, diagram his setup for me, and suggest ways I can get in there."

"Wait a minute here." He held up his hand. "I know enough about his setup to tell you getting in there is next to impossible."

"But not completely," she pushed. "Right?"

He rocked in his chair, lips pursed.

Jesse, who had been sitting quietly this entire time, shifted his glance between the two of them. "Can't be any worse than sneaking up on Taliban terrorists who shoot at every whisper of wind. If you lay it out, I know you can find a way in. But if you want to eavesdrop, you'll need some special equipment."

Alex concurred, a thoughtful look on his face.

"How often has he brought a group out here over the past year?" Terry asked.

"I'd say about every three months. He flies them in by helicopter, and they keep to themselves. They aren't what you'd call sociable."

"I wouldn't expect them to be. Morgan is probably continuing to indoctrinate them into his militia philosophy and hatred for the government that he feels has wronged him. I'm telling you guys, these people are insane fanatics. They'll do anything to destroy this country and make a political statement."

"I have to find a way to get in there," Terry insisted. "It is critical I know what they have planned."

"Then let's figure out how to do it," Alex told her. "I'm sure the fence around the place is electrified, and they've got a high-end security system to protect them from intruders." He looked at Jesse. "Here's where that SEAL training comes in. Plus, I'm not too crazy about Terry running around out there by herself."

"Damn it, Alex." She smacked a hand on the arm of her chair. "What's with all you testosterone-filled men? I'm a crack shot, and I've had every bit of the same training the other agents got. You and my boss think I can't blow my nose by myself."

"That's not it. If you were a man, I'd say the same thing. You know how dangerous these guys are, and I've heard plenty of rumors. I wouldn't want anyone going in there alone to scope it out. Put your ego aside and use your brain."

Terry bit her lip to keep from saying something stupid. Alex was right, just as Max had been. Doing this by herself was sheer stupidity. Why had she ever thought otherwise?

"He called you," she said. "Max Jaeger."

"Of course he did. I'd do the same thing. He has all the confidence in the world in you, but you have to have backup. Period."

"I'd like to lay this all out and go over things with you," she told Alex.

"Good. You only gave me sketchy details, so start from the beginning."

HOW AM I going to handle this?

While they took a short break, Jesse refilled his

coffee mug and stood at the kitchen counter, taking a slow sip. The last person he had ever expected to see when he hit the road for Montana was Terry Fordice. The universe was definitely playing jokes on him because no matter how he tried, he hadn't been able to get the woman out of his mind. Or out of his dreams. He couldn't count the nights he'd gone to bed dreaming of her naked in his arms, his lips closed around one taut nipple. Or his tongue stroking the wet slit of her sex, or his teeth biting her swollen clit. Or his cock sliding into the hot clasp of her body. At night, lying in whatever bed he occupied, his dick would be so hard he became addicted to cold showers and an expert at jerking off.

Not to mention the memory of the most erotic motorcycle ride of his life.

But it wasn't just the sex. She was smart and bright and funny. He could talk to her about anything. Well, almost anything, he corrected himself. There was that ruined piece of himself that he chose not to share with anyone, certainly not with Terry. He didn't think he could stand for her to think of him as damaged goods. She deserved so much better. So, like a coward, he'd run and tried to wipe her out of his mind.

But the joke was on him, because no matter how hard he tried he could not seem to get her out of his mind. Or eliminate the longing for her that ate at his gut every day. Now he was going to be sharing this house with her, a really nice house, older but well-maintained. The kind of house that would make a nice place for a couple. Only in his shape he'd probably never be a couple with anyone, especially ATFE agent Teresa Fordice.

"I'm a fucked-up mess," he muttered. "Who the hell would want me, anyway?"

"Do you spend a lot of time talking to yourself?"

Terry's voice startled him, and he nearly dropped his mug. As it was, hot coffee splashed on his hand.

"Shit."

He set the mug on the counter, shaking the liquid from his hand into the sink then running it under cold water."

"Sorry." Terry moved to stand beside him. "Didn't mean to startle you, but I wanted more coffee. Didn't know you were deep in self-discussion."

Jesse cursed silently. Now, on top of thinking he was an uncaring shithead, she'd get the idea he was a nutcase. Great. And he was supposed to work with her, back her up on this. He'd be lucky if she trusted him to open a car door for her.

"Sorry." He dried his hand on a dish towel. "I probably spend too much time alone."

"I guess you must enjoy your own company more than anyone else's."

He knew she meant it as a joke, but there was a bitter edge to her words that cut into him.

I am the stupidest fucker in the world.

"Not really." He forced a smile. "Let's get back to business."

He followed her back to the dining room where Alex Rossi sat looking at the diagrams they had drawn. He looked up at them.

"You guys having a problem or something?"

Jesse shook his head. "Not at all. I was a little clumsy with my coffee, is all. Okay, let's look at this thing again."

Just as Alex had said earlier, Reed Morgan's property was cut like a rectangle from a much larger ranch. Alex had brought his laptop and used it to access aerial photos of the area.

Terry studied them. "I'm surprised you got to take shots of the place."

"The U S Forest Service has helicopters. They map the areas so they have parameters if a fire breaks out. Couple of years ago we had a bad one in the Crazies and had to evacuate some of the ranchers and their people. The Forest Service likes to keep things updated just in case."

"Good idea," Jesse approved.

"You can see Morgan's place right here." Alex tapped the tip of a pen on one photo.

"This gives us a chance to see the entire layout." Terry traced her finger along a fence line. "I'm guessing, like we said earlier, this whole fence is electrified."

Alex agreed. "Plus, a high-tech security system."

"So how do we get onto the property without being seen and without being electrocuted?"

"Okay, we have an option. Morgan orders his food supplies from a store in Eagle Rock. I'll contact them in the morning because if he's bringing in a bunch of people he'll have to feed them."

"Wouldn't he order from Bozeman or Billings?" Terry asked.

Alex shook his head. "Not anymore. He pays the price because he thinks it gives him more control."

"So how does that help us?"

"Because we can hide in the truck." Jesse was the one who answered. "It's the best way onto the property."

"We have to figure out what to do from there," Terry reminded him.

"Then let's start throwing ideas out there and see what we come up with."

It was the first time Jesse had been in a work situation with Terry, and he was impressed with her laser-like focus. She knew what her goal was, and she was damned well going to find a way to get to it. And fast. But working with her was going to be a test of his inner strength. He had no idea how she felt about it. Or him. She had been coldly polite on the highway, at first even trying to refuse his help. Well, not that he could blame her.

It was apparent this was a critical situation for her and that was a priority. But how was he going to spend however much time with her and not remember both the time they'd been together and the coward's way out he took? The question was, could he get past the barriers she'd obviously thrown up?

He was on what had to be his fifth cup of coffee when there was a knock on the front door. It opened, and Zane Halstead walked in. Jesse stood and, when Zane walked over to him, the two exchanged a man hug. Jesse took a step back and studied his friend, and for the first time in forever thought there just might be a chance for him to be whole again. Or at least whole enough to make a life for himself.

Zane smiled. "Good to see you. Glad you made it here."

"Back atcha." He indicated Terry. "Meet Terry Fordice, an, uh, old friend."

Zane glanced from Jesse to Terry and back again, curiosity stamped on his face.. "So you two know each other?"

Jesse tried to shrug off his discomfort. "Neither of us expected the other to be here. Talk about coincidence."

One corner of Zane's mouth tipped up in a grin. "I think that's the story of life. Nice to meet you, Terry. Hope we can help you with your situation."

"Me, too, because otherwise I think we're in for a whole world of trouble." He glanced at Alex. "How far did you all get?"

"Just to how we'll get on the property and manage

to sniff around." He cast an eye at his watch. "Might think about some dinner, though. I didn't realize it was this late. Let me call Micki and see what she's arranged."

"All taken care of," Zane assured him. "She and Lainie should be here any minute with barbecue takeout."

Jesse was stunned at the easy relationship between the men. Alex was an unknown quantity to him, but if Zane had connected with the sheriff like this, then Jesse needed to keep an open mind about the guy and his offer. Helping Terry with her assignment would give him a first-hand opportunity to find out about the area and how Alex Rossi ran his operation.

"That's great," Alex was saying, "because I'm starved. Meanwhile, how about sitting down and seeing if you can help answer some of these questions. You've developed a pretty good picture of the area since you've been here."

Sitting next to Terry and concentrating on the task at hand was one of the hardest things Jesse had ever done. He was hyperaware of her body, her thick brown hair that she'd pulled back into a ponytail, the very faint scent of jasmine that clung to her, probably from the shower gel she used.. How the hell was he going to share a house with her and keep his hands to himself?

By reminding yourself what a mental and

emotional wreck you are and why you shouldn't foist yourself off onto someone.

Besides, after the way he literally ran from her life, why the hell would she want anything to do with him, anyway?

When the two wives arrived, they greeted everyone, shook hands with Terry and Jesse, and set about putting out the food. For the first time since he'd left the SEALs, Jesse Donovan felt as if life might have something to offer him and he could return the favor. He knew he could help Terry with this, ferret out what was going on, and bring down the bad guys. After all, that was what he'd done for a living.

But could he resurrect what had been an electric personal relationship? He damn sure was going to try.

CHAPTER 7

IT WAS nine o'clock by the time they called it quits. Terry had memorized every one of the photos, a benefit of a photographic memory, more technically known as an eidetic memory. She couldn't even take credit for it. It was something she'd been born with and often as much a curse as a blessing. Both she and Alex had notes stored on their laptops, and they'd discussed the next steps until every T was crossed and every I dotted.

"No room for mistakes here," Alex reminded her.

"Don't I know that," she agreed. "Whatever he's planning is going to be a disaster of epic proportions if we can't figure out what it is and stop it."

"I've been checking things out ever since you called, sniffing the scene, so to speak. The last I heard is that Morgan will be here tomorrow afternoon. People have been arriving in groups for two days, dropped off by a helicopter. I've had a good vantage point to watch it all without being seen."

"You said before that he usually orders from the local grocery store when he brings a group here, and they stock his pantry and freezer."

"That's correct. Emery Belzer will customize an order for him and handle it any way he wants," Alex explained. "And won't be letting comments drop to people about it. The latest supplies are supposed to be delivered early in the morning and stored before the man himself arrives. His order is five times what it usually is, so your information that he's moving his entire group there is probably correct. He's got a caretaker on the property who handles that. If we follow our plan, it will give you a chance to get inside the house, see who's there now, and plant your little bug. That is, if you can do it without raising any eyebrows."

"Oh, I can do it," Terry assured him. "I always find a way."

Alex smiled. "You always did get the job done."

"Let's hope this isn't an exception. I need to get on that property and inside the house."

She and Jesse would arrive at the grocery in time to help load the delivery truck. The store owner, a man named Emery Belzer, owed Alex a major favor, although he'd nearly wet his pants when pressed to agree to this.

"Although he wasn't too happy about it," Alex told

them. "He kept repeating if Morgan found out he did this, he'd be a dead man. He kept protesting when Alex called him to double check on everything. I had to assure him that would not happen."

"But he might be in danger, right?" Jesse asked.

"Anything is possible. I suggested stashing him and his family in a safe house until whatever the asshole's got planned is over. Or stopped."

"What did he say?"

"That he wanted to talk to his wife first. But in the end, he'd had no choice but to agree. He did say he and his wife were going to leave town immediately after. He wasn't taking any chances. They'd stay away until whatever this was had blown over."

"So, tomorrow you'll pick up Jesse and me and take us into town and the plan will begin."

"That's correct. And now we are all out of here. You guys need to get some rest. Tomorrow the countdown begins."

Now Terry just wanted a shower and bed. She was tired and achy and her head was full of unanswered questions. Jesse had insisted she take the master bedroom that had its own bath.

"Ladies get privileges," he joked. "Seriously. I'm used to roughing it." He waved a hand around the space. "Although I don't think I'd call this roughing it, no matter where I sleep.

She laughed. "I hardly think having a separate bathroom falls in that category but thank you."

Tension still crackled in the air between them, and the pull of a sexual attraction still so powerful she could almost see it. She had no idea what was going to happen with them alone in the house, or if Jesse would even say another word about the way he'd left. She needed to put that out of her mind. If they were going to be operating as a team, which she had to agree was a good idea, the last thing she needed was a distraction. In fact, neither of them needed it.

She was standing on the back porch, inhaling the fragrance of the night air, when she heard the door behind her open and close. The porch floorboards creaked under the weight of Jesse's steps. He didn't touch her, but he was so close she could feel his breath on the back of her neck.

"I'm sorry."

His voice was so soft, she wasn't sure at first if she'd heard what he said. She waited to see if he spoke again.

"I'm sorry," he repeated. "I was a real shithead."

She wanted to turn to him but wasn't ready to look at him yet.

"Yes," she agreed. "You were. I didn't deserve it."

He rested his hands on her shoulders then turned her to face him. For a moment she resisted, then she moved so they were facing each other.

"Terry," he began, and stopped.

"Why did you?" she asked. "Leave, especially the

way you did? Did you think your baggage was too much for me? That I wouldn't understand? Or want to help you?"

"Like I told you on the highway, I was too much of a fucked-up mess. Still am, come to that." He raked the fingers of one hand through his hair. "We had some bad shit over in Afghanistan. Really bad. I didn't handle it too well. Actually not well at all."

Terry forced herself to look into his eyes, shocked by the pain she saw there.

"And you didn't think you could talk to me about it?"

He looked away. "Terry, I didn't think I could talk to anyone about it. I'm just glad the nights we were together I didn't have one of those fucking nightmares."

She took a breath, reaching for the right words to say.

"Jesse, it takes a lot to frighten me. And just maybe I could have helped you."

"I didn't want to chase you away."

Her jaw dropped. "So instead you did the running? How does that make sense?"

"I wanted to leave you with good memories."

She put her hands on either side of his face. "So instead you walked away from what we had and left me doubting myself?"

"I didn't—"

She touched her fingers to his lips then took a

step backward. "I'm too tired to do this tonight, Jesse. It's been a long few days for me, and tomorrow is going to be even worse. We're both professional enough we can work together. Let's see what happens when this is over."

She turned and walked into the house, half expecting him to follow her. When he didn't a heavy sadness came over her. Maybe they'd never get to work this out between them. It would help a lot if she hadn't fallen in love with him.

When she got to her bedroom, she called Max Jaeger and laid it all out for him. She'd been dialing him in twice a day as he'd requested. They'd spoken before she met with everyone, and he'd agreed this was the best way to proceed. She could get a good look at the setup at Morgan's house and on his land and see if anything of interest popped up. He had checked Jesse Donovan out after the first time she'd called and told her he had excellent creds.

"I feel better having him team up with you," he told her. "Neither Rossi nor Zane can go in with you. They're too well-known, and Morgan will wonder what the sheriff's office is doing checking out his house. And I wasn't too happy with you doing this alone or with an unknown."

"It'll work, Max. I can snoop without appearing to and see if I can get a handle on what this is all about. I have a really bad feeling about it."

"Me, too." He paused. "Listen. I'm going to try and

get word to my source who's deep undercover with Morgan and see if he can get any information to you. It's tough for him to get the word out without breaking cover, and the last time he said he should know shortly what this was all about."

"Okay. I'll try to figure out how to make myself accessible to him."

"Call when you get back from there."

"Of course."

Disconnecting the call, she stripped off her clothes and tossed them onto a chair in the corner. She pulled a new sleep shirt out of her newly-purchased bargain suitcase and carried it along with a pair of bikini panties into the bathroom. Turning on the shower, she waited for the water to heat.

She had just stepped in under the steaming spray when the shower door opened and a very naked Jesse Donovan stepped into the steam with her.

"Jessie," she began.

"Just listen," he begged.

"Listen to what? Excuses? Lies? Why you betrayed what we had between us?"

"I don't want to," he told her.

She pushed her wet hair back from her head and blinked against the water.

"Don't want to what?"

"Wait until this is over. I know it's my own fucking fault you feel that way. I was an ass. I freely admit it. In fact, I haven't thought of much else since then but I don't want to wait another minute."

"Another minute for what?"

"This."

She was so startled she didn't move when he cupped her cheeks and pressed his mouth to hers. The contact was at once both new and familiar. For a brief moment she resisted.

Stop this. You can't trust him. He'll break your heart again.

But the touch and taste of him woke up slumbering memories that jolted to life. The shape of his mouth, his firm lips, the way he molded them to hers woke up every dormant hormone in her body. When he traced the seam of her mouth with the tip of his tongue, she opened for him and slid her own tongue over his.

Just this once, she told herself. Just something to keep her company on the lonely nights when she still missed him so much.

And just like that, despite what had happened between them, his sudden departure, his silence all this time, she wanted him just as badly as she had the very first time. And the last time.

When he lifted his head, she could see so much emotion swirling in his eyes.

"I'm sorry. I—"

She touched fingertips to his lips.

"Sssh. Later. Not now."

She brushed his dripping hair back from his face and lifted her mouth to his again.

Not even the water could cool the heat of the next kiss. It scorched her all the way to her toes. Her nipples hardened and tingled and between her thighs her hungry sex throbbed with need.

The kiss was endless as they explored each other's mouth, reclaiming a familiar taste. Jesse stood with his body pressed against hers, every muscular outline and curve of bone imprinting themselves on her. And his cock. Oh, yeah, the incredible cock, so long and big and thick. The remembered feel of it inside her hot, wet sheath jumped to the forefront, and she had to squeeze her thighs together so she didn't lose it standing right there.

Jesse was still doing a sexual dance with her tongue when he slid his hand over her shoulder and slowly down her back. His fingers tap-danced on her spine until they reached the very bottom of it. Then he eased just the tips of those fingers into the crevice between the cheeks of her butt. At the touch she automatically clenched against the intrusion but didn't pull away from him.

"Still just as hot and tight?" he murmured against her mouth, stroking and probing.

"You tell me," she teased in a shaky voice.

"We'll find out," he promised. "But I have other things in mind, first."

He moved his hands around to cup her breasts,

gently kneading them and brushing his thumbs over her nipples again and again. Each time he touched her, that same arrow of heat shot straight to her core, making it clench with need.

And all the while she could feel the thick, hard outline of his cock.

This is a huge mistake. He'll just walk away—no, run away—like he did before, and I'll be left putting myself back together.

It's worth it, her other voice shouted. *Shut up and enjoy.*

When she tried to press closer to him he eased her back an inch or two.

"There's no rush. I've waited a long time for this, thinking I'd never get it again. I want to enjoy every minute."

He pressed a kiss to the side of her neck, taking a tiny nip then trailing his lips across to her shoulder. The erotic feel of his mouth sent shivers down her spine and a soft moan rolled from her throat.

"Feel good, baby?"

The rasp of his voice was like a caress itself.

"Mm hmm. Everything you do feels good."

And wasn't that the damn truth.

Jesse squeezed her breasts again before lowering his head to close his teeth around one nipple. The bite was just sharp enough to send a bolt of pleasure straight to her core, and she had to squeeze her thighs together against the growing demand inside her body.

He knew just how to touch her, how strong to make that touch, how to bring her to that threshold where the pain gave so much pleasure. When he'd teased and tormented one nipple until she thought she couldn't stand it anymore, he moved to the other and gave it the same treatment. Her legs had trembled, and when she gripped Jesse's forearms to steady herself, he just backed her up to the tiled wall and continued his sensuous onslaught.

Then he proceeded to lick and kiss his way down her stomach, pausing to trace the curled flesh of her navel before moving his tongue to the pouty lips of her sex. She waited, holding her breath, for him to delve his tongue inside but instead he kissed a path up the inside of one leg and down the other, deliberately bypassing the one spot she desperately wanted him. The kisses were so light they were mere teases, setting every nerve in their path on fire.

Terry gripped Jesse's shoulders to steady herself, moaning in a combination of pleasure, need, and frustration. Her inner walls were spasming with the hunger for his cock to ease in there, yet still he continued to taunt her. When he finally pressed open the lips of her sex, she wanted to shove herself against his mouth and beg him to lick and eat every inch of her.

But slow was what he'd said, and slow was what he did.

He licked the wet slit from top to bottom and back again, pausing each time to give her throbbing clit a flick of his tongue. Each one brought a gasp of pleasure from her. She rocked against his mouth, held steady by the grip of his fingers on her hips. He licked and teased again and again, until she was sure she'd come just standing right there.

"Please," she begged, crying out her need.

"Please what?" he growled. "Please this?"

He spread her lips wider and took her clit between his teeth. Gently biting and tugging. She was so on the edge but she wanted more. Much more. When he moved his hands to slide two fingers inside her, she almost cried with relief. Rocking her hips back and forth, she rode his fingers hard, the friction ratcheting up the wave of pleasure inside her. He eased in a third in and stretched her wide, curling those fingers each time he dragged them out so his nails caught that hot spot that made her cry out in response. But when she tried to push down harder on them, he pulled his hand out.

"No!" she cried out in frustration.

Jesse gave that rough laugh again then rose to his feet.

"The first time I make you come after all this time I'm going to be inside you, so I can feel you grip me and milk me and hold my cock tight with your body."

He reached to the soap dish for a condom she hadn't even noticed him place there and rolled it on that thick, magnificent shaft.

"Now we're ready."

Nudging her thighs apart he wrapped the fingers of one hand around his shaft and guided it to her entrance. Even as aroused as she was, he was so thick —God! She remembered that incredible thickness!— that he had to ease himself in slowly, one fat inch at a time. By the time he was fully seated inside her, she almost felt as if he filled her to the top of her head. He gripped her hips to steady her.

"Look at me, Terry," he commanded, lifting her just enough to complete the penetration and hold her in place. "Open your eyes and look at me. And wrap those gorgeous legs around me. That's it."

She wound her legs around him and dug her heels into the base of his spine, locking her ankles together. When she looked into his eyes again this time, instead of pain she saw need and hunger and lust, and some emotion she didn't even want to try and name. And then there was no more talking. He began the slow in and out glide, back and forth, thrust and retreat, the width of his cock scraping against her walls with each movement.

She never took her eyes from his, never looked away. She saw the hunger increase with each movement, felt sharp spears of heat stab through her, lighting fires in every point of her body.

In and out. Back and forth. Slow and steady at first then faster and faster.

And all the time he talked to her.

"That's it, that's it. Jesus, you're tight. You are so fucking tight. You feel so fucking good. God damn, Terry. You are so fucking hot and wet. Yeah, that's it. Move like that. Oh god. Oh god. Oh Jesus. Come for me, Terry. Come right fucking *now.*"

He shouted the last word and, as if he'd pulled a trigger inside her, the orgasm that had been building so deep roared up like a hurricane and exploded. She anchored herself against him as spasms rocketed through her body while her inner walls milked his shaft with steady contractions.

She had no idea how long it went on, but at last the tremors faded away, leaving them both limp and exhausted. And sated.

Finally, she managed to uncross her ankles and ease her legs down until they touched the shower floor, but they were so shaky she wasn't sure she could stand.

"I've got you," Jesse said in a soft voice.

He wrapped his arms around her and held her against his body while their breathing slowed and their heart rates returned to normal. At last he leaned her against the wall and took the bottle of shower gel someone—probably Micki—had left in the soap tray. Without saying a word, he poured some into his hand and began to smooth it gently on her skin

"I don't know how you even have the strength for this," she told him with an unsteady laugh.

He looked at her and grinned. "Me, either, but I didn't want to miss this."

With lazy strokes he covered every inch of her body with the sweet-smelling lather, first her front, then her back. When his soapy fingers slid into the crevice between her butt cheeks again and the tip of one finger pressed against her opening there, he gave a very soft laugh.

"I want that," he told her. "Again. And we'll get there."

"Jesse," she began.

He turned her back to face him and shook his head. "Later. When we have time."

He soaped himself up with a speed she figured he'd learned in the military then rinsed them both off. He dried her first then sat her on the closed lid of the toilet while he took care of himself. He even dug a hair dryer out of her suitcase, and a brush, and amazingly enough, did a decent job drying her hair. Then he lifted her and carried her into the bedroom, ripping back the covers on the bed.

There was no question of them sleeping in separate rooms. He got her into her sleepshirt and bikinis she'd left on the bed and grabbed a pair of boxer briefs for himself. Then they were lying in bed together, her body cuddled up against his, his arm around her waist. She felt as if she belonged here, regardless of anything else.

But what happened next? They had a critical mission to perform and probably very little time to do it. And could she trust her feelings for Jesse? Or his for her?

"We've got time," he murmured, as if he could hear the thoughts in her brain. "And this time I'm not running anywhere."

She hoped he meant it. And before she could think anything else, she was sound asleep.

CHAPTER 8

I<small>T WAS</small> full dark by the time everyone gathered again at Reed Morgan's house, and he wasn't happy with what he was hearing.

"We're on the hunt," Curt Renshaw told him. "Haven't stopped but so far none of our contacts have been able to tell us anything. They all have her picture and description. They've reached out to their own people but continue to come up empty.

"So, you still have no idea where she's gone to?"

He stared at Renshaw in disbelief. The man always knew where everyone was. Sometimes his ability to locate and identify people was scary even to Morgan.

"I've hit everyone one of our usual contacts everywhere. She hasn't popped up in any place. It's as if she disappeared off the face of the earth."

Morgan curled his hand into a fist and clenched it

to control himself. This was just not possible. No one could disappear without some trace.

Not true, a little voice whispered. You know people who have done that.

But they made elaborate preparations and planned ahead of time. Was that what this bitch had done?

Set this up knowing she'd need an escape hatch? Who the fuck was she, anyway? He glanced at his desk calendar. Today the last of his group was being moved to the ranch. They'd be flown in, just like the others, at night when people were home and not out riding open land where the helo could be spotted. Tomorrow he'd arrive himself, in the open, as he'd done many times.

He'd already placed the order for supplies. He needed to feed the men, especially as hard as they'd be training. Over the past year he'd had truckloads of arms delivered a little at a time, so arming his group was not a problem. He had a fleet of helicopters ready to transport them to their individual destinations so they'd be ready at Zero Hour. And he had the final run-through all set for the key group on the day before Zero Hour.

This country wouldn't know what hit it. It would be in a shambles, and he'd be able to step in and steer it in the right direction. He was tired of being ignored or labeled a radical or a nutjob or any of those labels. Now they'd have to listen to him and he could get rid of all the assholes steering the country in the wrong direction.

But first he had to find that bitch of a magazine writer, or whatever the fuck she was, and erase every trace of her. He'd reached out to every source at his disposal today with zero luck. How the hell could one female just disappear into thin air? Had a hole opened up in IH-75 and swallowed her and her car?

Renshaw had taken note of the auto rental agency sticker on her windshield the first day she arrived at Morgan Arms Manufacturing He'd called them from his car the minute he lost her and asked them to check the GPS locator on it. They told him it had gone stationary in Austin. When they tracked it, they found it in the parking lot of a strip center in Austin. The keys were under the front seat and the car had been wiped clean. Their little portable machine had not picked up a single fingerprint.

Well, that was certainly fucked.

He wondered if Beckett had had any better luck tracking her down. In a way he hoped not. Just one more thing for the man to rub in his face. On the other hand, the man's connections made Morgan's look amateurish and ineffective. Still, in and of itself it was an embarrassment. Something else Beckett could hold over his head. That was becoming a habit Morgan needed to shortstop or he'd have yet another benefactor to eliminate.

How was it possible his life was falling apart like

this, and at such a crucial moment? He'd planned for something like their Zero Hour project for a long time. He lived and trained his men with military precision. He eliminated people who disagreed with him or might prove to be a problem. He'd covered every single base. Except. One. It made him sick to think he'd been so lax abut Terry. All the reports he ran on her had come back verifying her story, but he knew he should have looked harder. Dug deeper.

But as good as Morgan's very talented hacker was, Beckett had one even better. He'd told Morgan about it right after Renshaw's report that morning, throwing a phrase over his shoulder that made Morgan's stomach clench.

"I'll find her. I've got a man who can find anyone. And find their history."

Yes, he thought now, somewhere there would be a trace of this female, and Beckett's man would find it. Much as he hated the man who discovered who she was, it was still time to call him and see what, if anything, he'd found out. Just as he picked up his cell to call the man, the phone rang and Beckett's number appeared on the screen.

"Tell me you have something," Morgan snapped.

"Oh, I've got it all right," Beckett said in his gravelly tone. "But you won't like it a bit."

Morgan clutched the cell tighter in his hand. "What the hell is that supposed to mean?"

"It means that your little girl is a government spy.

That's what it means. It also means we could be fucked if we don't take care of her."

Morgan rubbed his jaw, trying to gather his self-control. This was one of the rare times in his life he'd let his ego get the better of him. He'd never do it again.

"How the hell did you find out? I had people digging with virtual shovels."

"I have better shovels than you do. But you could have found out before if you checked her hotel."

Morgan frowned. "What do you mean?"

"If she hauled ass out of the city, what happened to her stuff at the hotel? You knew where she was staying. You could have found someone to bribe the way I did who'd let you know when someone came to fetch her stuff."

"And?"

"And sure enough, someone came to clean out her room. My guy got a shot of the car the cleaner was driving and tracked the license number. It came from a car rental business. Enough money changes hands and you get what you want. The guy who took care of everything is a government agent."

Morgan wanted to put his hand through a wall. He was losing his edge and at the worst possible time.

"Fuck," was all he could say. "Just goddamn fuck."

"Here's a thought," Beckett told him. "What if somehow the government we all hate so much got a sniff of what's being planned and sent her to you to see what she could find out?"

"Impossible," he snapped.

But was it? He had vetted every single person in his "army." Those who didn't pass muster were eliminated. He couldn't risk loose lips, but somewhere there had been a leak.

Just fuck it all.

"I'll find her," he told Beckett.

"No." The other man growled the word. "I'll find her, and I'll take care of her. You just keep your shit together and don't fuck up Zero Hour."

Morgan wanted to deck the man. He'd had the same problem with Vanetti only with a different slant. Give a man too much monetary control and he thought he owned you. Vanetti wanted him to change his philosophy. Beckett wanted to be in charge. All he needed was another week and he could get rid of Beckett, too.

"I'm moving the last of the men to Montana tomorrow," he told the other man. "Do you want to fly out with me?"

There was a short silence. "No. I'm staying right here. In case something goes wrong I have to have plausible deniability."

"Nothing is going wrong." Morgan gritted his teeth. Then he inhaled a deep breath and forced himself to let it out slowly. "Everything will go as planned."

"It damn well better. Keep me in the loop."

The call disconnected, and Morgan was left sitting there holding a dead phone.

When this is over, and I'm in control of everything, all Beckett's wealth isn't going to stop me from blowing this man out of the water.

He pulled up a list on his phone and studied it, mentally checking off each item. Okay, time to move the troops.

"No!"

The shout woke Terry, the sound of a man's voice laced with pain. Despite being tired, from the tension of the situation, two days of driving, and some of the best sex she'd ever had, she came awake instantly. Jesse was sitting up in bed next to her, his body rigid.

"Jesse?"

"Where's our cover? Where the hell is our damned cover?"

She reached out to gently touch his shoulder and had to duck as he swung an arm in her direction. Okay, he was having a nightmare, totally unaware of his surroundings, his mind back in Afghanistan, which had been his most recent assignment before his discharge.

"Fire! Right now!"

She had to wake him up before he did damage to himself or her.

She slid to her feet before turning on the lamp on the nightstand, standing away from the bed, just in case. Then she waited a minute to see if that would wake him up. After a minute he blinked and turned toward where she was standing, confusion and panic warring in his eyes.

"Jesse." She spoke his name in a soft voice. "Jesse, can you wake up for me?"

"They're dead." The agony in his voice was painful to hear. "Oh god, they're dead."

"Jesse," she tried again.

"Dead." He buried his face in his hand.

The sound of his sobs was so agonizing it actually hurt her heart. She had to find a way to wake him up.

"Jesse." She raised her voice. "Jesse, it's okay. Wake up. Come on, wake up now."

She was afraid to touch him again, but the sound of her voice must have penetrated the fog of his nightmare. He turned his head in the direction of her voice, and blinked twice. Somehow she had penetrated the veil of the nightmare.

"Terry?" His voice sounded as if he was strangling, and he repeated her name. "Terry?"

She pressed against the side of the bed, reached out and touched his arm, jerking her hand back at once, just in case. But this time he didn't swing at her, turned his head toward her and blinked again. Then he dropped his head into his hands.

"Terry. Oh Jesus. I am so sorry."

Believing he was in control of himself, she climbed back onto the bed and stroked his arm.

"Are you fully awake now?"

He didn't say a word, just nodded.

"Okay. Good. I'm going to get you a glass of water."

By the time she came back from the kitchen carrying the drink, he looked as if he'd pulled himself together, at least somewhat. He accepted the glass and drank down half of it before setting it on the nightstand. Then he patted the bed next to him.

"It's safe for you to sit here." He tried for a smile. "The crisis is over, at least for now. I won't be attacking you anymore tonight."

She sat close to him and took one of his hands in both of hers, stroking it lightly.

"You startled me," she said at last. "I worried you'd hurt yourself."

"Or hurt you." He said that in a flat voice. "Now you know why I hightailed it away from you. I never know when I'm going to get one of these. I could do some serious damage to you. I could never live with myself if that happened."

"There are ways to deal with it, you know." She continued to stroke his hand. "Have you seen someone about this?"

He snorted. "You mean a shrink? When I finished my tour and did not re-up, they wanted me to see someone, but I've never been very good about sharing my feelings." He glanced over at her. "I grew up learning you kept that shit inside you. People didn't want to hear it, so you just manned up."

"Tough father?"

He shook his head, and a corner of his mouth tilted a little. "Tough mother. She could put a BUD/S instructor to shame. Oh, she had her reasons, but it left its mark on me."

"You need to do it," she told him. "If you want to do more with your life than see the country on your motorcycle, that is."

"Right now I need to figure out how to keep my shit together so I don't fuck up this operation. I'd never be able to live with that. Alex is including me based on Zane's recommendation, and I don't want either of them to be sorry."

"I don't think either of them would be. They wouldn't include you so easily if they were."

"But—"

"But nothing. This is a great chance for you to prove to yourself that you can keep it together. And after this is all over, I want you to seriously think about talking to someone to get you past all of that."

When he didn't answer that, she just squeezed his hand and slid back under the covers. Eventually he lay back and pulled the covers over himself, too. He resisted at first when she tried to get him to spoon her, but finally he blew out a long breath and curved his body around hers.

"I want to make this work between us," he said at last in a low voice, his breath tickling the back of her neck. "I just don't know if I can. If I'm too damaged. My being here is probably a bad idea all around."

"Not at all. Not even a little. So, like I said, let's take care of this and then we'll see what's what."

When he didn't' say anything for a long time, she figured he wasn't going to answer her. Then, out of the darkness, he said, "I'm going to try. For you. Okay? Let's get some sleep. We have a busy day tomorrow."

He tightened his arm around her, and she fell asleep with her lips curved in a smile.

CHAPTER 9

IT WAS cold in the morning, with a hint of frost in the air. When Zane came to fetch them, he grinned at Terry huddled into her jacket.

"Winter comes early in the Crazies," he told her. "Glad you brought a warm jacket."

She'd looked up the temperature when she'd stopped at the big box store to replenish her wardrobe and supplies. She'd never been a fan of real cold weather, but she'd learned to tolerate it on some of her assignments. She'd made coffee as soon as she got up, and she and Jesse both were cradling mugs in their hands.

"As long as there's plenty of hot liquid," Terry said, "I'm good."

"We can arrange that."

The three of them managed to fit in the large cab

of Zane's pickup, and shortly they were on the road heading into Eagle Rock.

"You like it here?" she asked Zane.

He grinned. "I do as long as Lainie's here."

Terry smiled "Good answer. But, outside of that. You like it as a place to live? Like your job?"

He thought about it for a moment. Did he know she was asking the questions for Jesse? Did Jesse sense it?

"I wasn't sure when I got here," Zane told her finally. "But I wasn't handling my problems too well where I was, even though I was living close to my sister and parents. I just didn't want them to see that flawed side of me."

"But—"

He shook his head. "Let me finish. Alex Rossi is an incredible human being, besides being one of the best SEALs and an extraordinary lawman. He's given people like me a chance to find ourselves again and have a purpose in life. Oh, he's plenty tough about it. No room for error but plenty of support while you're getting there."

"Interesting."

"And, of course, having Lainie in the picture when I left Tampa gave me someone to focus on besides myself. It's her story to tell, but maybe she'll open up to you. Anyway, once I got here, I realized this really was a good place to regenerate yourself. Lots of fresh air, beautiful scenery, great people for the most part. And Alex has a good plan to give new focus to those SEALs who are having trouble fitting back into society. We love it here."

Jesse had not commented through the whole conversation, but she sensed he had paid careful attention to it.

And speaking of paying attention, she was startled to see they had turned off the highway into the little town of Eagle Rock. At this hour of the morning there were hardly any people moving around, but when they turned down another street she spotted a big square building that seemed to be all lit up.

"That's our destination," Zane told her. "We'll pull around back to the loading dock and get things squared away."

At the rear of the building, a big delivery truck was backed up to the dock, its rear doors opened, and three men were moving cartons from that truck to a smaller one parked next to it. Zane parked and turned to his passengers.

"Ready?"

Jesse nodded. "I'm good."

"As I'll ever be," Terry added.

When they climbed up to the open dock, Zane introduced Terry and Jesse to the man holding a clipboard and checking things off. Emery Belzer looked as if he'd rather be anywhere but here. He looked at Zane with a bitter expression on his face.

"I hope your people know how to move cartons,"

he spat. "if they damage any of this stuff, Reed Morgan will peel the skin off my hide in strips."

"No problem," Zane assured him.

Belzer looked at Terry. "You didn't say there'd be a woman. She doesn't look like she can handle a handkerchief."

"I'll be fine," Terry assured him. "I can bench press two hundred pounds."

Belzer looked as if his eyes would pop out of their sockets but he just gave a grunt of agreement.

"Really?" Jesse whispered in her ear.

"No, but I wanted him to think so. Let's get to work."

Alex had told them exactly what would be expected of them, so Terry and Jesse got to work loading all the cartons Emery Belzer had marked to transfer. A man named John Anderson, put in place by Alex, would drive the truck to Morgan's place. Alex told them the man was a local who had no love for Reed Morgan or any of his ideas he'd heard. Alex had made a connection with him, and Anderson was more than willing to haul supplies to Morgan's place and do a little spying now and then. Also, by now, Morgan's people were used to seeing him as an occasional driver, so it didn't raise any red flags.

Before long, they were ready to go. Terry sat in the middle between John Anderson and Jesse as they drove out of town and down a winding road to the entrance to Reed Morgan's place. She recalled what it looked like from the aerial shots, but this gave her a chance to see it up close and personal. Rolling grassland stretched out on either side of the narrow road that led to the house itself. To the left and right of the property she could see cattle grazing on the neighboring ranches, but there was nothing on Morgan's except the long building that she knew was the firing range behind the house.

They stopped at the gate in the fence that enclosed the property, and John reached for a phone in a metal box attached to one of the bars.

"We're here with the delivery," he told whoever answered.

In a moment the gates swung open, and they drove through. They had barely cleared it before they swung closed again. Anderson drove the truck around to the rear, and they all climbed out. When the back door to the house opened two men, both very tall, dressed in jeans and flannel shirts, walked out onto the porch. One of them held a clipboard and nodded to Anderson.

"Morning, John. Your turn into the delivery barrel?"

Anderson dipped his head. "Something like that."

The man frowned at Terry. "You got a woman on your crew this time? Can she handle it?"

"She needs the money and, yep, she's good. Works out with weights."

The man studied Terry for a long moment,

assessing her. "Okay, then. If you say she's good, she's good."

"You got your inventory sheets?"

"Right here." The man lifted his clipboard. "We'll check everything off as your crew brings it in. You know how Reed can get if things aren't just so."

"Indeed. All right, let's get to it."

Terry and Jesse worked silently, unloading the boxes and waiting for them to be checked off before bringing them inside on the hand trucks. They were directed to place them in a big room filled with shelves to the right of the door. As they brought in the cartons, men who had been waiting unpacked them and stacked the goods on the shelves.

"You'd think he was going to keep us here for a year," one of them choked as he unpacked cans of soup. "I thought the big day was happening before next week."

Terry saw the other man shoot him a look and step on his foot, a signal to be quiet. So, the target date wasn't far away. Did he plan to bring people back here afterward? They needed more information. She wished she could get farther into the house. Alex had given her a tiny but powerful listening device, but she had to find a way to plant it. They certainly weren't going to do much talking in the oversized pantry closet.

"Excuse me." She stopped near the man without

the clipboard. "Is it possible there's a bathroom I could use?"

He studied her face for a long moment as if searching for lies before he turned.

"Follow me."

He took her through the kitchen down a long hall that led to a big living room. There was a small bathroom on the right.

"I'll wait for you," he told her. "In case you get lost finding your way back to the door."

She forced a smile. "Thank you."

Although she couldn't see much of it, she got the impression the house was as large as it looked from the outside. Sprawling, with many rooms, and a second floor she was sure was all sleeping quarters. Plenty of room for the men he had sent here. She stayed in the bathroom a sufficient amount of time before flushing the toilet and running the water in the sink. She had noticed a little table against one wall in the short hallway, and when she came out of the bathroom she deliberately tripped and fell against it, catching herself by gripping the edges.

The man waiting for her grabbed her elbow "Watch it. You okay?"

"Yes. Fine." She flashed a smile. "Just a little clumsy. Thank you."

And inventive, she thought. She'd managed to stick the tiny listening device to the back edge of the table, hoping it would pick up what they needed.

Additionally, she caught glimpses of a large group of men also dressed in jeans and flannels in the living room and dining room. None of them looked friendly, and they all appeared to be studying some kind of document. When they heard her, they looked up, saw one of the so-called helpers was with her, and returned to whatever they were reading.

"Okay. Let's go."

The man with her tugged her in the direction from which they'd come and was right on her heels as she made her way to the back door. By now all the cartons had been brought in and the dollies wheeled back to the truck. One of the two men doing the unpacking reached out and shook her hand.

"Thank you for delivering everything," he told her. "Mr. Morgan makes sure we're well fed."

"Good." She shoved her hand in her pocket. When he'd released his grip, she'd felt something stick to her palm, and she didn't want to lose it.

"Let's go, people." Anderson motioned them back to the truck and climbed into the driver's seat. "We've got more work to do today."

Morgan's people stood in silence while Terry and Jesse got back in the truck, staying on the back porch and watching before turning to go back inside the house. Terry figured they'd been monitoring them either through a window or the security system, however, because, as they approached the gates, they swung open to let them through.

No one said a word on the way back to town. Terry wasn't sure how much John Anderson knew, so she didn't want to say anything in front of him. Instead she maintained her silence and kept her hand in her jacket pocket, making sure whatever was stuck to it was safe. At last they were back at the grocery store where Zane was waiting for them.

"John, you know to make yourself scarce for a few days?" Zane reminded him.

"I do. No problem. Helen and I been planning to head to Arizona for a week to see the kids, anyway. We fly out this afternoon."

"Good move." He shook the driver's hand. "Have a great time and don't hurry back."

They said goodbye to John and climbed into Zane's truck.

"This way if someone mentions a woman on the delivery team," Zane told them, "and Morgan has any idea it might be you, he can't get hold of John to ask him."

"You think he knows I'm here?" A chill raced along her spine.

"Terry, I think Morgan can find out anything he wants. We're not taking chances."

"Oh. Of course. Thanks."

"Something wrong with your hand?" Jesse asked her, noticing the awkward way she'd moved with her hand in her pocket.

"Nope. Hold on."

She opened her hand slowly and saw a SIM card —a subscriber identity module— stuck to her palm. Holy shit.

"What's that?" Jesse asked.

"Max Jaeger said he had a source deep undercover with Morgan's group. I'm pretty sure that's the guy who shook my hand today. He gave me this. Zane, get us back to the house fast. And can you call Alex to meet us there? I might as well see what's on this when everyone's together."

By the time they reached the house, Alex was there waiting for them, with his laptop.

"I know you have yours here," he told Terry, "but I thought we might need two."

"Always glad to have extra," she agreed.

She pulled out her cell phone, took out the SIM card and replaced it with the one she'd been given. The she hooked it up to her laptop and began to upload what the card contained. As text scrolled across the screen, they all stared, mesmerized. When the last bit of information was uploaded, Terry turned to the others. Alex and Zane had shocked looks on their faces.

"What the hell?" Terry looked from one to the other. "What is this? What's Malmstrom? You mean the Air Force Base? You think they'd try to blow it up? Easier said than done. And would it make the statement he wants?"

Alex spoke up first. "Malmstrom Air Force Base is

one of only three bases that continues to maintain and control the Minuteman III ICBM. The Intercontinental Ballistic Missile. It's part of the Air Force Space Command in Colorado."

Terry frowned. "I've heard of them. Who hasn't? But I thought all the missiles were decommissioned or buried or something."

Alex shook his head. "All but a few still alive at Malmstrom and two other bases. This particular missile has a range of 3,400 miles and carries a nuclear warhead."

Everyone stared at him, the silence so thick Terry thought she could actually feel it.

Finally, Jesse cleared his throat. "Do you think Morgan is insane enough to try and steal one of those missiles?"

Alex rubbed his jaw. "Stealing one is not the problem. You can't get it out of the base without the proper transportation plus the codes to unlock the silo. Plus, you have to go through so many layers of security to even get to it I don't see how it's possible. But more

than that, you can't haul a missile away in any kind of secrecy."

"I don't think they want to steal it," Jesse told them. "I'm guessing they want to aim it somewhere."

Again, there was heavy silence as they each absorbed the possibility.

"Those missiles are heavily guarded," Zane

pointed out. "And not exactly out in the open. You'd have to get through a secure gate then be able to proceed from the gate to the first silo. Enter the small building housing the elevator. Punch in codes to take you down to the surface where the missile itself is located. Then remove the operators on duty, have the launch codes, and make it happen. Do you realize how impossible that sounds?"

"Improbable," Alex corrected, "but not impossible. You can buy anything with money if you have enough."

Terry snapped her fingers. "Beckett. Lyle Beckett. I asked Max Jaeger to find out everything about him and how he's connected. He's got enough money to pay off half the military if he had to."

For a long moment, no one said a word. The prospect of what they were discussing was so frightening they hated to even give voice to it.

"All right." Alex looked at them. "Let's move forward as if this, as unbelievable as it is, could really happen and that's on Morgan's agenda. What can we do to stop it? And fast because you know things are poised to roll any minute."

"Terry." Zane looked at her across the table. "Can you get your boss to help us with some facts we'd need? Like entry to the part of the base where the missile are stored? How long it takes to actually launch? And what kind of human protection is provided?"

"I can do that. But let's make a list of everything we need to find out and then regroup here. "

"Good," Alex agreed. "Let's get moving. We don't have much time."

"Let me call Max right now, and we can start there."

As with every other call she'd made to him, Max answered on the second ring.

"Go," he said.

"We have a situation," she began.

"Hold on. Let me get to my office. At the moment I'm in a meeting room with other people."

Terry waited, impatient, until Max came back on the line.

"Okay," he said let's have it."

She told him about her trip to the Morgan property that morning, including the large number of men there.

"Something big is about to happen," she told him.

"Did you manage to hook up with our guy?"

"He made it happen. And, Max, this is going to scare the shit out of you."

She told him everything that had been on the SIM card his man had passed to her. For the first time in all her conversations with him, Max Jaeger was dead silent on the other end of the connection.

"Jesus, Terry," he said at last.

"Exactly what we all said here. Max, we can't do this by ourselves, but you can't deploy an army here, either. We don't want to signal Morgan we are onto him."

"You're right. Okay, give me a few minutes here. I have to take this higher on the food chain, but I will call you back as soon as I can. Hopefully within a half hour. Stand by."

"What did he say?" Alex asked the question the moment she disconnected the call.

"About what I expected. This is beyond his pay grade. He has to reach higher up, and he'll call me back within thirty."

"One of the most critical pieces of information," Jesse pointed out, "is knowing

when they plan to do this.

"We're all agreed on that," she said. "I know Max will want us to keep an eye on the place. Alex? Zane? Is there a place we can do this without exposing ourselves."

"Yes. I think there are a few. Let me pull up the different county maps. Terry, I'll send you the links so you can pull them up, also."

In seconds they were all hunched over the two laptops studying the images on the screens.

"I've got a couple of suggestions," Zane began.

"Hold that thought," Terry told him as her phone beeped. "Here's Max." She punched Accept. "What did you find out?"

"That this is a big fucking mess." His voice was harsh and tight, the way it always got when he was faced with a critical emergency and someone had fucked up.

"Someone took a payoff," she guessed.

"That's it. What pisses me off is that people in other areas knew about this weeks ago and never passed it along to our agency even though we had a watch on him. They were using the creep for bait to draw out Morgan and his top men for a bigger sweep." Max snorted. "He's lucky we didn't kill him ourselves. I can promise you heads are going to be chopped off for this. The director is out for blood."

"How did he find out?"

"He put pressure on some people, and one of them got nervous and caved."

She felt sick. "Tell me if I'm right. Morgan's money man, the former or the present, paid someone to give him diagrams of the missile sites, the schedule of the teams who guard them, and the codes for the security gate, the elevator, and the missile itself." She swallowed. "Holy shit, Max. That's treason!"

"Believe me, that person—and his superiors—are being stuffed in a dark box as we speak."

"But that doesn't remedy the situation. Listen, right now we're looking for a vantage point to keep an eye on Morgan's place, but when is this disaster supposed to occur?"

"Sometime within the next three days," Max said. "That's as close as I could find out at the moment. But here is the worst part. The target?"

"Yes?"

"Washington, D.C."

Terry was afraid she was going to throw up. My god!

"And of course, the best way to destroy the government."

"Right on." Max cleared his throat. "Listen, I am headed into a meeting with some of the top brass who are then headed to the president's war room. Find a place to keep watch. I'll be sending troops to back you up, but I'll call, and we can figure out the best way to do this under the radar."

"Okay. I'd say thanks, but I don't know what I'd be thanking you for."

"Later."

Alex stared at her. "What?"

When she related what Max had said, every face at the table turned pale.

"Fuck." Jesse spat the word. "Fucking assholes. Fucking shithead assholes."

"I'm with you," Zane agreed, "so let's do our part to stop them. Alex, I think I've figured out a location where we can keep an eye on Morgan's place. Terry, pull up the topographical map Alex sent you the link to."

"Got it," she told him.

When he explained his idea, they all agreed, although putting someone in that spot was going to take a lot of maneuvering.

"We can use the helicopter," Alex agreed, "because most of the ranches in that area have one so its appearance won't raise any eyebrows. But we need to plan the drop carefully."

"Okay." Jesse dipped his head. "I'm in for whatever you need. Let's do it."

"This isn't exactly what I had in mind for you, Jesse," the sheriff told him, "when I had Zane contact you."

"Are you kidding? This is the most alive I've been in ages."

"Yeah, well, good on that, but it's not like that around here all the time."

Terry sneaked a look at Jesse and saw him grin.

"I've been here less than twenty-four hours," he told them, "but it's already growing on me. Now. Let's get down to business."

CHAPTER 10

REED MORGAN CLIMBED down from the helicopter after it landed at his place, rage and frustration boiling inside him. Lyle Beckett had given him information that made him want to shoot everyone in sight. That fucking bitch Teresa Franklin—no, real name Teresa Fordice—worked for the fucking ATFE. They'd sent her to dig out information on him and find out what he was up to. How had he missed that?

Because I let my fucking ego get in the way. I thought the magazine was seriously going to do a profile on me and give me the creds I wanted.

Yeah, he'd never do that again. And it pissed him off that Beckett was the one who'd dug it out.

But that wasn't the worst of it. Beckett had also discovered that the Fordice bitch was here in Montana. And right here in the Crazy Mountains. Was nothing going his way? He'd tasked Curt

Renshaw with finding her exact location and getting rid of her. He wasn't giving Beckett any more power over him.

Why did the money men turn out to be so power hungry?

Frank Vanetti had been the one to pay the guy at Malmstrom to shoot him the diagram, the schedule, and the codes. Then Frank had wanted to be top dog when the thing went down, and Morgan had worked too hard for too long to let that happen. Morgan told Ed Gooding who as second in command wasn't giving up anything to anyone, and that was the end of Vanetti.

Now Lyle Beckett was proving to be another problem. He guessed the people with the most money always wanted to have the most power. He had three days to make sure the plan was solid together and keep his army in place and up to speed and with himself as the recognized top man. He'd do it. After that, it would be his show all the way.

Meanwhile he had to get his shit together and not be distracted in any way. This event was too big to blow because he wasn't paying attention. He'd worked too long and too hard for it. Selected and trained his men. Believing the only way to fix the government was to destroy it and then rebuild it, he'd put this master plan together, and they were within days of accomplishing it.

Floyd Gorman, the man in charge of training at

the house and keeping people on track, came out to meet him, and they shook hands.

"Everything okay?" Morgan asked.

"As planned. Come on in."

He followed Gorman into the house, Don Emery right beside him. With Renshaw off searching out Teresa Fordice, Emery was serving as his bodyguard. With things the way they were, he wasn't going anywhere, even his own houses, without his private security. He wasn't sure who he could trust anymore.

In his private study, he dropped into the chair behind the desk and turned to Gorman.

"How's everything here really? The truth. We're too close to Zero Hour to have any loose threads."

"The men are working hard. Their proficiency at the range is practically perfect. When we follow up in D. C. with boots on the ground, they'll have no trouble nailing anyone who gives them trouble."

"Good. Very good. And the training?"

"They're in tiptop shape," Gorman assured him. "Couldn't be better."

"Excellent. That's what I like to hear."

"I told them that this afternoon you'd be giving them a little pep talk, and they're excited about it. I figure we could do it at the range. It's the only place big enough to hold everyone."

Morgan's mouth curved in what for him passed as a smile. That was one of his favorite things to do, speaking to his troops and sharing his philosophy and goals with them.

"And the pantry is stocked? We need enough for this entire group for the next three days, and you know how hungry they get."

Gorman nodded. "Delivered this morning."

"Anderson drove it out?" Two different drivers changed off bringing the deliveries to them. He'd checked them both out, and nothing had rung any alarm bells.

"Yes, he did. And his people had it offloaded and into the pantry in record time."

"Yeah? Who did he bring this time? The two guys from the last delivery?"

"No." Gorman shook his head. "Newbies again. More day workers looking to pick up extra money."

Morgan set his briefcase on a table next to his desk, opened it, and took out some folders.

"As long as they do the job."

"They got it done." He chuckled. "Had a woman on the crew this time. I wasn't sure she could haul that stuff, but she sure kept up."

Morgan paused, a chill racing through him "A woman?"

"Uh huh. Not bad looking, either, if you like that type."

"What type? Floyd, what type is that?"

"Oh, you know. Dark hair, big eyes. Not too tall. I like the tall, skinny blondes myself."

The chill settled in Morgan's bloodstream.

"Call Emery and ask him what her name is," he directed the man.

"Reed, it's just a broad hauling groceries," Gorman assured him.

"Call him," Morgan insisted. "Now. Humor me."

Gorman pulled out his phone, found the number, and punched it in. He held the phone to his ear for a long time, frowning as he listened.

"That's weird. There's a voice mail message. Says he and his wife are off for a couple of weeks on vacation."

"Was that his landline? Call his cell."

Again, Gorman got no answer. "He's got his cell on voice mail, too."

Morgan ground his teeth. "He's made himself scarce."

The other man looked puzzled. "But why? What for? And what's such a big deal about this broad?"

Careful, Morgan told himself. Don't let anything on to the people here.

"Call the store and ask for the names of the people on Anderson's team today. Humor me, Floyd. Okay?"

But the owner of the store was in Bozeman, the clerk who answered the phone told them.

Morgan wanted to bite nails. It was that bitch. He just knew it. Somehow, in the next couple of days, he'd find her and cheerfully kill her. He wasn't going to be stopped now, when the goal was so close.

He punched the speed dial on his phone for Renshaw.

"Any news yet?"

"No, but I'm still working on it."

"Find her and bring her to me, before our deadline. I want to deal with her myself."

"HE's HERE."

"Saw the helo when it came in," Jesse answered.

Alex had decided—and the others agreed—that Zane should be the one placed to watch Morgan's property. He knew the area. Jesse would be parked a few miles away, hidden in a copse of trees where people driving by would not spot him, and receive the updates. He, in turn, would notify Alex if action of any kind was needed. And Terry would go with him, bringing her computer to monitor the listening device she planted and also look up anything either Jesse or Zane might need.

They were severely shorthanded if things ramped up. Alex still had vacancies on his staff, but he had reached out to the county and asked for support if he needed it. He explained they had a situation where a resident may be causing trouble, without giving out details. They were as prepared as they could be without knowing what next steps Morgan and his crew were going to take.

It had taken some doing to get Zane into a place without his approach being seen and where he could still be hidden, but they'd managed to work it out. Now he was settled into a sheltered spot in a niche of the mountain Morgan's spread bumped up to, watching for anything taking place on that land. Jesse was a half mile away, obscured from view by a thick copse of trees, ready to pass any information back to Alex. They'd both been in their spots for the better part of an hour.

Terry sat beside him, huddled into her warm jacket and grateful for it. A cold spell had suddenly blown in, and she hadn't wanted to waste either the time or money driving to Great Falls to shop.

"I can do all the shopping I want when this is over," she'd told Jesse, who chose not to argue with her.

Her responsibility was to monitor the bug she'd placed in Morgan's house. She had her computer balanced on her lap, picking up anything at all that came through, but so far the conversation had been pretty neutral.

Jesse glanced over at it. "I wish we'd get more out of that thing."

She frowned. "You think they might actually suspect?"

"No." He shook his head. "I think it's just been

drilled into them to be careful no matter where they are. But they do keep referring now and then, casually, to Zero Hour. I'm guessing that's the name of this project. If we only knew what the actual Zero Hour time was, it would be a help."

"Maybe they'll talk about it more now that Morgan's here."

"Let's hope. So far we got nothing but garbage as he walked in and went to a room where we heard him close the door. Probably his office there."

"We'll just keep listening and hoping."

For Jesse, it was like one of his SEAL reconnaissance missions, except the company was a lot better. Sitting next to her like this, so close, was doing funny things to him. He kept reliving the previous night with Terry, pulling out every precious moment as if it might be the last.

And then there had been his fucking freak-out, the nightmare that plagued him and wouldn't let go. He kept seeing the bomb explode when part of his team was killed. The ambush when they'd gone to extract a high-value target and deliver him for questioning and imprisonment. The attack by the Taliban when they were on a recon mission.

And more, and more, and more.

It seemed as if the scenes were never ending, burned into his brain and rolling at will like an old-fashioned movie reel. He'd tried outrunning them on his motorcycle, but that hadn't worked. Counseling didn't appeal to him. He couldn't see spilling his guts to someone who hadn't been there and experienced the horrors he had. Burying himself in the body of a nameless female seemed to be the only thing that helped, but that was way too temporary.

His only peace had come during the time he'd been with Terry. The only nightmares he'd had were on the nights they weren't together. But what if he had them when she was there, like last night. Sure, she hadn't run screaming or kicked him out of bed, but how long would that last? How long would she put up with it?

His mind drifted as they sat in the truck, so close he caught the faint scent of the cologne she'd dabbed on this morning.

He'd woken again, just before dawn, the remnants of the nightmare teasing at his brain. He was afraid if he went to sleep again it would take hold as it had before so he forced himself to lie there, awake.

Terry had been sprawled next to him, her head on his shoulder, one graceful hand resting on his stomach. He didn't realize she was awake until she spoke.

"Dream trying to come back?"

What should he say? Yes, and have her throw him out of bed? No, and lie about it? Then he'd felt her hand sliding over his abdomen, caressing him.

"Your muscles have muscles," she teased, stroking the hard plane of his abdomen, her touch driving him nuts.

"I'll show you muscles," he drawled, placing her hand directly over his dick.

She squeezed it gently, her thumb creeping up to stroke the smooth skin of the head. He was instantly so hard he was afraid he'd come before they ever got to the good parts. But when he tried to move her hand away, she just squeezed him tighter and bent to string kisses over his chest.

"My turn to make you feel good."

She closed her slim fingers around his hard shaft and began to move her hand up and down in slow strokes. He forced himself to lie there, letting her do her thing, feeling as if he should be making her feel good, too, but enjoying the hell out of this. Her slender hands were both gentle and strong at the same time, squeezing and stroking as his cock swelled and throbbed.

He threaded his fingers through the silky mass of her hair, thinking about guiding her head down to work with her hand when she rose to her knees and, as if reading his mind, closed her hot, wet mouth over the swollen head.

"Oh Jesus!"

No one had ever made him feel the way she did. Hot and cold at the same time, aroused, totally immersed in the moment and the act.

As she ran her tongue around the head, she continued to caress his shaft with one hand while sliding the other between his legs to cup his balls and squeeze him.

Shit! Shit! Shit!

He was so close to coming, he had to work had to back off. He didn't want this to end. Maybe ever.

She hummed against his dick, the vibrations reverberating through the flesh, one hand squeezing his balls while the other stroked him up and down. He lost himself in the rhythm, the heat surging through him, the softness of her touch.

His orgasm exploded with unexpected force. One minute she was working him slowly and evenly, his body building to the big finale, the next it could not seem to wait one more second. It roared up from deep in his body, exploding into her mouth as she sucked and stroked and squeezed. He was unaware of anything except this incredible woman and her ability to lose himself in her and find a peace that eluded him everywhere else.

It felt as if he came forever, Terry sucking every drop into her mouth and swallowing as she continued the magic with her hands.

And then he was done. Finished, totally depleted.

Terry lifted her head, cleaned the head of his cock with her tongue then smiled at him.

"Think you might be able to sleep now?"

"Oh yeah." He wound his fingers through her hair. "I—" He stopped. "You—"

"It's okay." She placed a soft kiss on his lips. "I wanted to do it. I enjoyed it, too."

She slid down next to him, pulled the covers over both of them, and rested her hand on his chest.

"Better get some shuteye. We've got a big day tomorrow."

And surprisingly, when he closed his eyes, he fell asleep at once.

"Jesse? Jesse, are you okay?"

Soft hands were tapping his face, trying to rouse him.

Fucking shit. Did he fall asleep?"

He rubbed his eyes.

"Jesus, Terry. I can't believe—"

She touched her fingers to her lips. "It's okay. You had a sleep-deprived night." She grinned at him, then her face sobered. "But it's almost time for Zane to check in again. I figured you'd want to be awake for that. "

He rubbed his hands over his face, pissed at himself and embarrassed.

"Sorry. I don't know what happened. I never, ever fell asleep on the job."

"It's okay," she assured him. "You know I'm here if anything happens. And I think you really needed this. I'm glad you feel relaxed enough with me that you can do this."

"I think you turn my head upside down," he told her.

"That's okay, as long as it makes you feel good." She wet her lips. "Listen, Jesse, I—"

He held up his hand to stop her. "Not here. Not now. But when this is over, I want to talk."

She hesitated a moment but then agreed. "Okay. But we both get to say our piece, right?"

"Of course. Just think about this. I can't walk away from this again. Somehow I want to find a way to make it work. To make you trust me that I'll stick this time. We have something good here, and I'm scared I'll fuck it up again."

"Not if we work together. But let's get through this first."

"Jesse?" Zane's voice crackled in the headphone.

Jesse held it so both he and Terry could hear.

-"They all just left the house and headed for the gun range. There must be forty men there, plus Morgan and his personal crew. I think he's taking them for a pep talk."

"Too bad we couldn't bug that building."

Zane chuckled. "Yeah,. That would have been great. Well, let's just watch and see."

"You have enough coffee?" Terry asked.

"Oh yeah. Lainie gave me enough to keep me awake until next week."

Terry laughed. "She takes good care of you."

"That she does. I'm a lucky man." His voice softened when he spoke of his wife.

Terry, who had learned their story from Alex,

personally thought Lainie was the lucky one. She wondered if Jesse would ever conquer his problems the way Zane had. Well, that was a subject for another day. Meanwhile, they had an urgent situation that required all their concentration.

CHAPTER 11

AT FIVE THIRTY in the morning, Terry was awakened by a text from Max.

"We have more information. Trouble. This is no longer a solo operation by an agent out there alone."

"I told you, I'm not"

"I mean with agency personnel. I'm on the way and arriving with a team early a.m. Best place to meet up?"

She texted him back and tried to go back to sleep, but her brain would not shut off. At last Jesse, roused by her tossing and turning, urged her to get up and they'd have coffee.

"I think we're done sleeping for the night anyway," he told her.

At seven, she texted Alex to let him know Max was flying in from D. C. with a team and their expected time of arrival. Max had told her they'd arranged for their own ground transportation, and she'd told him to come directly to the house where she and Jesse were staying.

By seven thirty a.m. the three of them plus Zane were gathered around the dining room table. Even as early as it was, they were far from sleepy. In fact, sleep was the last thing on anyone's agenda.

"Any more from your boss?" Alex asked.

"No. I thought they might text when they landed." She looked at her watch. "Could be any time now according to what he said. Let's get started, in the meantime. We can talk about the measly info Jesse and Zane collected yesterday."

"Okay." Alex looked around at each of them. "Just to review. The original word we got was that Zero Hour would take place in the next three days. One day has passed, so that leaves today and tomorrow. Anyone have any suggestions how we can narrow this further, since the bug doesn't seem to be picking anything up?"

"I don't—" Terry was cut off by a new voice.

"Yes. I do."

No one had heard the front door open and close, so they were startled to see the tall man in military fatigues striding into the room trailed by six others in similar dress. He glanced at Terry.

"Nice to see you, Agent Fordice."

"Ditto, Max." She turned to the others. "Let me

introduce you to ATFE Special Agent and my boss, Max Yeager."

Max shook hands with everyone then turned back to Terry.

"I have news that none of you are going to like."

Her stomach knotted but she didn't panic.

"Let's go into the living room where there's room for all of us."

But despite adequate seating, Max's team chose to stand, silent, while he gave them what he'd learned.

"First of all, we've wrung everything we can out of the traitor who gave out the codes and the information about security teams scheduling. The fact we identified him is being kept secret so Morgan won't find out his plan is blown."

"And is it?" Jesse asked. "Are you able to stop it?"

"Yes." The word was clipped and firm. "One of the things we're doing is allowing the traitor to remain at work, but we have two armed guards watching him, and one of our top programmers checking everything the guy does on the computer so he doesn't send any coded messages to Morgan."

"Smart," Alex told him. "And impressive."

"Do you know when Zero Hour is supposed to launch?" Zane asked.

"Yes. tomorrow morning. Eight a.m. is Zero Hour. We believe they picked that for two reasons. One, that is the start of the business day in D. C., when the most people will be in the capital. The missile would destroy not only the entire city but miles of the surrounding area. And the nuclear fallout would extend even beyond that."

Ice crept down Terry's spine at the words, and nausea bubbled up in her throat. This would devastate this country and put it in a totally disorganized and damaged condition.

"Morgan could just sweep in with his men and take over. That's the main reason he's been ordering larger quantities of material for manufacturing. He's been stockpiling weapons for their takeover of the capitol. And other places."

"They'd have to wait for the nuclear fallout to disperse before they moved in," Max pointed out, "but the country would be in such a shambles it wouldn't matter."

"So what can we do?" Jesse wanted to know. "What's the plan? What's *their* plan for getting to a missile?"

"As I said, they're making their move tomorrow morning. At eight o'clock there is a regular guard change for the missiles. Their plan is to wait just before the gate that leads into the compound, waylay the team, and move in themselves. They think they have the codes for the missile that our traitor gave them so they believe they are all set."

"Don't the guards at the gates know who to expect?"

"The faces change so much because there are so

many different people involved, they only ask for credentials and match the faces to the photos on the passes."

"And the plan is?" Alex prompted.

"My team and I will get there far in advance and conceal ourselves in the thick trees across the road. Morgan's people plan to arrive about seven forty-five, set up a fake accident with bodies in the road, and when the guards stop to check on it they'll capture them—or kill them if necessary—and take their places. But we'll be waiting, and we've asked Malmstrom to delay the changing of the guard for thirty minutes."

"We want to be part of that," Alex told them.

"That includes me," Terry added. "I've been involved with this."

Max shifted his gaze to her. "Morgan has a price on your head. He's put the word out. His new money man, Lyle Beckett, discovered your real identity so he thinks he's in the driver's seat."

"You can keep me out of sight," she insisted. "I deserve this, Max. Please."

In the end it was decided the four of them would join Max and his people and, at seven in the morning, they would all head for the spot Alex indicated on the map."

"I got almost nothing from the bug," Terry told him.

"My guess is they have some kind of electronic muffler. It was worth a try, but it was a longshot."

"Well, damn."

They reviewed the plans with the entire team several times before Max was satisfied everyone had it memorized and knew exactly what they were supposed to do. The next step was to hide Max and his people until the morning.

"Our place," Alex said. He looked at Max. "My wife's family owns—"

"A big spread," Max interrupted. "I know. When I knew Agent Fordice's plans I had every one of you checked out top to bottom including your underwear. I have to say, it's comforting to know that we'll also have three former SEALs on the team." He turned back to Alex. "About that place to stay…"

"No sweat. I just texted my wife. The bunkhouse will hold all of you, and she plans to feed you."

"That's very kind of her. I'd also like to get a look at the setup near the gate to the missile silo. We can do some practice runs near the bunkhouse, if that works for you."

"Whatever you need," Alex assured him.

"Then I say let's get moving. Terry, you need to ride in someone's truck hidden beneath the dashboard. Beckett's got people everywhere looking for you, and we don't need to take any chances."

She wasn't about to argue with him. She wasn't

foolish enough to deliberately make herself a target. They left Jesse's motorcycle at the house and rode with Zane to Alex's place. He followed them there, introduced everyone to Micki, and went over the schedule with her. Terry marveled at the composure of the woman who had been through a horrendous experience as a teenager and then had to deal with her father's murder and the knowledge he'd been part of the group raping young teenagers like her. It was plain as day she and Alex were very much in love.

The woman was obviously pregnant, and Zane confided in her that although she worked for the county attorney's office, she was on a leave of absence until after the baby was born.

The day passed in a blur. Max and his team, joined by Zane and Jesse, worked on every possible scenario of the takedown. Alex did not include himself because he had the sheriff's office to run and county business to oversee. He would, however, be involved the next day. The air was filled with the tension of anticipation, and it seemed to take forever until the day ended and supper was served.

Everyone retired early, in preparation for the big day. Launch time for them was seven o'clock a.m. Terry demanded not to be left behind, despite the bounty on her head, and Max and Jesse got tired arguing with her.

"You're the one I'm worried about," Terry said.

She and Jesse were staying at the big ranch tonight so they didn't have to expose her to watchful eyes.

"I'm fine. I swear it." Standing in the bedroom they were sharing, the only light the moon coming in through the window, he cupped her chin and stared hard into her eyes. "Believe me. I would not take part in this tomorrow if I thought I'd have some kind of episode and put others in danger. That's not who I am."

"I worry about you," she told him.

He smiled. "It's nice that you do, but, Terry? Just so you know. I finally realized I was a fool to run away the last time. I see at last you aren't the type of woman to run away from a situation like that. I'm just a stubborn idiot, but I was also scared. Afraid of what you might think or feel."

"We'll have plenty of time to discuss that when this is over," she promised. "I don't want to ruin things either, Jesse. As long as we're truthful with each other, we can make it through."

They slept in each other's arms that night, silently agreeing to leave sex off the table until this whole mess was over.

Max was inside the house right after dawn but Jesse and Terry were both already up. Micki, complaining she needed to feel useful, was up fixing coffee and setting out muffins for everyone. No one had much of an appetite, and most of them, including

Jesse and Zane, said they never ate before a mission. And then it was time to leave.

Max's men had two big SUVs they were traveling in. Max had a big double cab pickup that the rest of them used, Terry again hidden beneath the dash just in case. The air was heavy with the kind of anticipation Jesse said they always experienced before a mission. Everyone was armed and carried extra ammo.

When they got to where the gate to the silos was, they split up, half going in each direction because they weren't sure exactly which one Reed and his men would approach from. It seemed like an eternity before they heard the hum of tires on the road and two jeeps, each with four men, came into sight. They both stopped and everyone but the two drivers got out. Terry recognized Morgan at once as he strode to the middle of the road..

"Run one of these Jeeps into the ditch," he ordered. "Bring the other one close, at an angle, and just have them touch, so it looks like an accident."

They all waited while Morgan staged the scene, then added five minutes for good measure. Terry remembered the real guards had been asked to delay their arrival by thirty minutes, but she was still nervous. Morgan, who had climbed back into one of the Jeeps and leaned sideways as if he'd been hurt, poked his head up.

"Gorman, what the fuck is going on? They're ten

minutes late. I thought you said you timed this enough to know their timing was precise."

"I don't know," Gorman answered. "This isn't right. Maybe—"

"No, it's not." That was Max's voice as he stepped out of the trees with his men. "Get your fucking hands up and do it now. I'd just love for you to give me a reason to put a bullet in you."

"What the hell?" Morgan looked around.

"Game's over," Morgan. Your little plan isn't going to work. D.C. is not going to get blown to hell today. Sorry."

Terry watched Morgan trying to decide what to do. The look on his face was a mixture of fury and disbelief. All those weeks and hours of planning, all the money spent getting the codes they needed to fire the missile, gone to waste. He sat in the Jeep, hands raised as he'd been ordered to do, while one of Max's team relieved him of his gun and checked him for other weapons.

"Out of the vehicle." The man nudged him with his own gun.

With all the other men also under guard and surrounded by Max, his team, Jesse, Zane, and Alex, she finally walked out of the trees to the scene on the road.

"Sorry to spoil your party," she told Morgan as she reached the road.

"You!" He could hardly speak as incoherent with

rage as he was. "You fucking bitch. I should have listened to Beckett and gotten rid of you at the beginning."

The guard standing beside him again ordered him out of the vehicle. So swiftly it caught everyone off balance, Morgan leaned forward then sat up holding a gun pointed at Terry, firing as he did so. Most of the bullets missed, but one of them nicked her arm. Before the man guarding Morgan could react, or Terry herself could fire, a bullet hit Morgan's hand, causing him to drop the gun. He screamed, cradling his arm, blood dripping from his injured hand.

Terry looked at where the shot came from and saw Jesse standing there, still bracing his gun hand, looking at Morgan with pure hatred on his face.

Max actually laughed. "Nice shot, Donovan."

"I should have shot the bastard in the head," he growled. "But then we wouldn't be able to show the world what a piece of shit he is."

"Is someone going to take care of my hand?" Morgan yelled. "I'm bleeding."

Jesse looked at him. "Tough shit." He hurried over to Terry and examined her wound.

"It's just a nick," she insisted. "Didn't even enter the flesh. Here.""

She pulled off the shirt she'd worn over a T-shirt and handed it to Jesse to wrap the wound.

"I about had a heart attack," he told her. "All I could think was how I'd been such a selfish ass, only thinking of myself and my problems and nearly missing out on the best thing that ever happened to me. I just didn't want to put that on your shoulders, you know?"

"I've got big shoulders," she told him, grimacing slightly as he tied off the material over the wound.

He smiled, but she could still see traces of fear in his eyes.

"I'm not running this time," he promised. "But we do need to talk about the future."

"I like the sound of that."

And despite the audience and the grimness of the situation, she stood on tiptoe and pressed a soft kiss to his lips.

By now, all of Morgan's men were cuffed and distributed in the vehicles so each was guarded by a heavily armed man. Max rode in the lead Jeep, sitting in the back next to Morgan whose hands were cuffed despite his wound. No sympathy there, Terry thought. She and Jesse once again rode back with Zane and Alex. At the sheriff's office, they were met by armed soldiers from Malmstrom. They all boarded a very large helicopter standing in the field next to Alex's office where more armed men were waiting.

"I'll call you," Max hollered at Terry as he ran for the chopper. The rotors were already turning. "Guys? Thanks for your help. We'll be in touch."

Then it was just the four of them again.

"We'd better let our wives know we lived through this," Zane said to Alex with a wry grin. "Otherwise we're liable to get shot ourselves."

"True that." He looked at Jesse and Terry. "You guys okay if we take off for a bit? We won't be gone long. And I know we'll have questions to answer here." He waved at the porch of his office where his small staff stared at them, curiosity stamped on their faces.

Jesse put his arm around Terry.

"I need to bandage her arm, and I think we both could use a drink." He looked hard at her. "And then I think we have a lot of things to talk about."

"Right." Terry laughed despite the pain in her arm. "So don't hurry on our account."

"I plan to do a lot more than talking," Jesse murmured in her ear.

"Is that so?"

"Uh huh. After."

"After what?"

"After I show you why you need to keep me around. And this time I'm not leaving."

EPILOGUE

THE STORY FILLED the news for several days. Frank Morgan was a nationally known figure, and while those who knew him were aware of his extreme views regarding the government, no one had expected anything like this. The thought of what the Minuteman ICBM could do to the nation's capital had a lot of people scared for a long time. And it had the government changing a lot of its protocols and background checks regarding the whole missile process.

Ed Gooding had been identified as the killer of Frank Vanetti. A former sniper, code name Deadshot, it had been an easy job for him. But Morgan, known as Steel for his iron control, had lost it over Lyle Beckett and wanted to do the deed himself, once Zero Hour had passed. He'd been heard to say he was sick of people using their money to try and push him aside. The men gathered at his place in Montana were also arrested although, since they had not committed an actual crime yet, they were all released. But the government planned to keep a sharp eye on what they did from here.

Terry had taken a leave of absence, which Max readily signed off on, and she and Jesse were using the time to get to know each other better and come to some decisions about the rest of their lives. They explored the area, spent some time with the Halsteads and the Russos, and a lot of time with themselves.

They had just finished a lazy morning of making love in bed and were seated on the back porch with fresh coffee, enjoying the view.

This was truly the happiest she'd been in a long time. She and Jesse had talked many long hours, about what had happened when they were together before and since. He had also spoken with Zane and agreed to start seeing a counselor to get some help with his PTSD. Day by day it seemed they were growing closer together. But they were also coming closer to having to make some decisions about the future.

"I think I could look at this forever," Terry sighed.

"Yeah?" Zane had his arm around her, and she rested her head on his shoulder, one of her favorite places to be. "Interesting that you should say that."

"And why is that, exactly?"

"Yesterday when I went into town I stopped by Alex's office. He'd asked me to come by for a few minutes. Said he wanted to talk to me."

Terry sat up. "About a job?"

She knew he'd been discussing the pros and cons at length with Zane.

"Uh huh. I'd have to take the classes at Montana Law Enforcement Academy to get my license, but he said I'm qualified to go right into the advance program."

She tried not to tense up. She knew Alex really wanted him, and Lainie Halstead, who she'd become friends with, had extolled the virtues of both the job and the area. The longer she stayed here, the more she liked it, but she was determined the first move had to come from Jesse.

"And what did you say?"

He shrugged. "I said it depended on you. I didn't want to be here unless you did. Terry, I screwed up a lot last time, and I've paid dearly for it. I don't want to live the rest of my life without you. I want to marry you and settle here in the Crazy Mountains and raise kids with you. But you have to tell me what you want."

She sat for a moment, realizing that for the first time in her life she felt really at peace.

"I want the same thing," she told him. "I trust you this time, Jesse."

"Hold on, then." He fished in the pocket of his

jeans and pulled out a little velvet pouch. Then he got down on one knee.

"Jesse?" She stared at him.

"I love you, Teresa Fordice, more than I thought I could love a woman. Make me the happiest man on earth and say you'll marry me? Please?"

She knew she could have drawn it out, but she had no reason or desire to.

"Yes," she told him, throwing her arms around him and raining kisses on his face. "Yes, yes, yes."

He managed to maneuver the ring free and slid it onto her finger then kissed her again.

"I have something to tell you," she said. "Max called the other day. Said if I didn't want to come back to Washington, there was an opening in the field office in Billings. It's a short commute, and he says the people there are very nice."

"A lot quieter than you're used to," he pointed out.

"And that's a good thing," she said. "I'm kind of getting used to quiet."

"Think we should go inside and seal the deal?" he asked.

"Our own Zero Hour?"

He smiled, a hungry look on his face. "It is."

Terry laughed. "I can't think of anything I'd rather do."

∿

If you have not read Book #1 in Heroes rising
Here is Chapter One of Desperate Deception

I also recommend you read Guarding Jenna and
Unmasking Evil

The two books that set the stage for the series

DESPERATE DECEPTION

Desiree Holt

A HEROES RISING NOVEL

Desperate DECEPTION

Hiding a strange woman was not on his agenda...

DESIRÉE HOLT

USA TODAY BESTSELLING & AWARD-WINNING AUTHOR

BROTHERHOOD PROTECTORS

CHAPTER 1

She was in a soft, warm, comfortable place, cocooned. Happy. She wanted to stay there forever, but a distracting voice kept talking to her.

"Come on, Lainie. Can you open your eyes for me? I want to check your blood pressure again."

The voice was familiar but the last thing Lainie Taggert wanted to do was open her eyes. The pain would come back, along with the feel of *his* fists and *his* voice raging at her. Here, in this darkness, she was safe.

"Please, Lainie?" the soothing voice begged again. "Come on. Open those baby blues. Just for a few minutes. I promise."

The voice was both familiar and nonthreatening, so Lainie gritted her teeth and forced her lids open. Well, at least one. And found herself looking at the face of Drea Halstead. The woman who had once been her friend, eons ago, before *he* had taken over her life and cut her off from everyone.

"There you go." Drea smiled at her. "We have to stop meeting like this."

"Drea?" Lainie tried to blink and realized she could only see out of one eye. "Is that really you?"

"Sure is. I only started here last month. Got a job offer I couldn't refuse."

"Oh god." A tear rolled out of her good eye. "I'm not dreaming, right?"

"Nope. When I got your chart and walked into this room, imagine my surprise to find my friend lying in this bed." Her lips curved in a hint of a smile. "I know we haven't seen each other in a good while, but, really, you didn't have to go to such drastic lengths to make it happen."

Lainie tried to move, but pain surged everywhere in her body, including her left hand. And her left arm seemed to be restrained in some fashion. She wanted to close her eyes again and fall back into the soft place where none of this existed.

"Nope. Uh uh." Drea's voice was both coaxing and demanding. "You have to wake up so I can talk to you." She paused. "What's going on, Lainie? I pulled up your hospital records. This has become a really bad pattern."

"I know." Lainie tried to hide her embarrassment, but she hurt too much to do anything but lie there. She knew she needed help, but where could she go?

Who could she turn to? This time was the worst. Next time he might kill her. "Drea, I—I don't—I 'm sorry."

"Stop. Please. You have nothing to apologize to me for. But that asshole you live with, the one whose goon told me to get lost or else, is going to have to answer some questions."

"Oh lord." Lainie closed her good eye. "Please tell me he's not here."

"He's not here. But, Lainie, you can't go back to that house. I'm afraid he'll kill you."

"You're right, but I don't know what to do," she whispered. "I have no one to go to, no one to help me, and I have to get away from him. God, Drea." She closed her eyes for a moment then opened them. "I don't know how a smart woman like me got herself into a situation that looks as if there's no way out."

"I wish I'd insisted you leave him when you had the chance. I've gotten so I can spot the abusers."

"But I didn't see it then," Lainie reminded her. "I still had blinders on." She swallowed back tears that were a combination of pain and humiliation. "I can't believe how stupid I was."

"Not stupid. Men like Sonny Fitzgerald are great con artists." Drea studied her.

"More than that," she whispered. "They're evil."

Something she hadn't discovered until too late.

Drea studied her for a long time, and Lainie

187

wondered if she had bad news to tell her? She wasn't sure she could take any more.

"What?" she asked at last.

"Listen," Drea went on. "I've been thinking about this a lot while you were being treated and lying in here. Lainie, I have a way out for you, if you're willing to take it."

Lanie stared at her. A way out? Was it even possible? "Like what?"

"What if I could make you disappear? Not only from the hospital. I mean from the city. And without Sonny Fitzgerald knowing how or where you'd gone to?"

"I don't know how you could do that." Lainie swallowed, although her throat was so dry it hurt. "He's going to find out where I am. He finds out everything. I had to use my cell phone to call for the ride here. I meant to get rid of it after that, but—" She caught her lower lip between her teeth.

"A cell phone I have in my possession, without a battery or sim card." She grinned. "I watch a lot of television. I'm talking about making you disappear from here."

"You can do that, even with my injuries?" Lainie was almost afraid to hear the answer.

"It's not as bad as it could have been. Your right eye is swollen shut, your face looks like a painter's palette fell on it, your left shoulder is sprained, which is why it's in a sling, and two fingers of your left hand are broken. The doctor taped them together to stabilize them." She paused. "And the rest of your body is sprouting brises like flowers in a garden, but all that will heal. We've got to get you out of here, so this doesn't happen again."

"When Sonny comes to pick me up, which you know he will, if I'm not here he'll pitch a fit." She closed her eyes for a moment. "Drea, I learned something I wasn't supposed to know. That's part of the reason he went berserk last night. Teaching me what would happen if I opened my mouth. He'll be insane to find me. What will you tell him?"

"We'll get to that in a minute. Look. We've been friends for a long time. We're still friends, despite the fact that asshole has cut you off from everyone but him and his people."

"I know, and I'm so sorry." She felt like crying, but this was no time for tears. She had to be strong.

"Forget that. This is your fourth visit here this year," Drea went on. "Honey, why didn't you ever reach out to the medical staff? They would have called the police and taken you to safety."

She wiped away a stupid tear with her good hand. This was no time for that. "He'd have found me, Drea. It wouldn't have been pretty for me or the people shielding me."

"But the police—"

"Can't always do what you want them to."

"He won't find out anything. I promise you. But,

according to Rick, the other times Sonny brought you he insisted that you fell, or some other half-assed answer. It was obvious he got you to go along with it or the police would have been called."

"You have no idea how angry that made him, that they wanted to report my injuries. If not for Geoff Miller, his driver/bodyguard, pointing out to him that if he made things worse, he'd be all over the news and possibly be arrested, he might have killed me when we got home."

Lainie could still remember the rage.

"But this time," Drea pointed out, "however you managed it, you got here by yourself. It's the perfect time for you to do a disappearing act."

"I know." The nausea came roiling back, and she swallowed again. "Could I have some water, please?"

"Of course." Drea held the paper cup with a straw up for her to sip. "Slowly, please."

"Thank you."

"It's a damn good thing you aren't married yet." She stopped and looked at Lainie. "You aren't, right?"

"No. I just—"

"Never mind. I've been thinking about this while you were getting patched up and drugged to make the pain a little easier to bear. I have a way out for you, and you need to take it if you want to stay alive."

Lainie tried to shift in bed only everything hurt even worse whenever she moved.

"But what? How? I'm desperate enough at this

moment to do anything, but what? Where can I go? No one will take me in, knowing what Sonny would do if he found out. I don't want to endanger them, anyway"

"Got it taken care of. I have someone who won't be afraid of Sonny and can get you out of here before that man even knows you're gone."

Lainie was almost afraid to hope. "Who would that be?"

"Remember I mentioned my brother, Zane, when we were still able to spend time together?"

"I do. The SEAL, right?"

Drea nodded. "Former SEAL. He's been medically discharged because of injuries from his last mission, but he's still in pretty good shape. Well, he's going to Montana to some rural area to get his act together. I'm going to get him to take you with him."

"What?" Lainie gasped. "But he doesn't even know me. Why would he do that? And what happens when we get there. Is he just going to leave me on my own? I can't—"

"Don't panic." Drea took her uninjured hand. "He'll make sure you're set up there, and he'll protect you, at least until you can make some decisions for yourself."

"He's not going to want to take a basket case like me with him." But god, on its own, a little hope wriggled through her.

"He will," Drea assured her. "I promise you he

will. SEALs are big into protecting people. US Navy SEALs are the most elite combat unit in the world, and they carry it into their personal lives."

"And what about when Sonny comes looking for me here, like he always does?"

"Rick will handle it while I make myself scarce. As far as that asshole Sonny Fitzgerald is concerned, you merely walked out of the hospital and no one saw you leave. Rick and I have it all worked out."

"You don't know Sonny," she protested. "He can turn on the charm one minute and cut your throat the next." She grimaced. "Too bad I saw only the charm until it was too late."

"We all do stupid things," Drea assured her. "Sadly, yours turned out to have danger attached to it. But you don't worry about Sonny Fitzgerald. Dr. Carvallo can more than handle him and give him plenty of misdirection. And he made sure my name doesn't appear anywhere on your treatment chart, in case he remembers we're friends."

"Drea?"

"Yes, Lainie?"

"Listen." How could she phrase this? "You should be aware of this. Sonny did something really terrible. Worse than just hitting me because he feels like it. If he finds me, I know he'll kill me." She stopped to take a breath. "And he could easily kill anyone who helps me."

"What did he do?"

Lainie squeezed her eyes shut. She couldn't tell Drea. It would put her in jeopardy, too.

"I can't tell you. But if it gets out—Anyway, I had a tiny window of opportunity, and I took it. But I have to get away. This is way more than his usual stuff."

Drea's mouth tightened, but then she squeezed Laine's hand.

"Then it's a good thing I have a fearless SEAL for a brother to take care of my friends."

"Are we?" she asked. "Still friends?"

"Honey, we will always be friends, no matter what. So. How about resting here for a few. I'm going to call Zane."

"He won't want to get involved with this," she protested. "I'm a stranger."

"Not to me. Now lie there and rest while I work things out."

"I—I don't know how to thank you."

"Letting me get you out of here is thanks enough. When I come back from my phone call, we have to get your stuff together. Then I want to give you a pill for the pain so you can handle the shifting around and walking out of here."

"I can pay him," Lainie said quickly. "I've been hoarding money, and before I managed to get out of the house this morning, I stuffed all of it into the pocket of my jeans. Will you check—"

"Already got it." Drea pulled an envelope thick with bills from her pocket. "And I can tell you he won't take a dime. But Jesus, Lainie. How long have you been squirreling this away? And how did you do it?"

"Six months." Lainie closed her good eye. "Pretty pathetic, right? Sonny didn't stop me from going to the grocery store, and I always got cash back. Not enough to raise his eyebrows when he checked the account."

"Lord, Lainie. Why didn't you drive to a police station? Or come to me?"

Lainie sighed, the effort hurting her chest. "He always had someone following me. And do you think the cops in this city would go against the great Sonny Fitzgerald? He's an icon. People fall all over themselves to curry favor with him. I still don't know how you're going to pull this off, even if your brother is stupid enough to agree to it."

"My brother is far from stupid, and, like I said, he's a former SEAL. Protecting people is their first order of business." She let go of Lainie's hand, placing it on the sheet. "Let me go make that call. Then I'll be back to get things rolling."

"W-What are you going to tell Sonny? I know he'll show up here when he discovers I'm gone."

"We're going to tell him you walked out of here and we have no idea where you went. Period." She handed Lainie a gel pack. "Meanwhile, hold this on your bad eye."

Lainie lay back against the pillows, trying not to

think about the pain and her dangerous situation. After his temper tantrum last night, Sonny had left her alone to crawl upstairs to their room. He hadn't even bothered to ask how she was in the morning, just told her she'd better heal herself because no more hospital visits. Then he dressed and left for his office. Thank the lord she was able to call an Uber and get out of the house before he came back to check on her.

When she'd first gone to work as Sonny Fitzgerald's paralegal, she couldn't believe her luck. She'd spent ten years at two law firms making herself the best paralegal possible, looking for a big break. And the same amount of time looking for her dream man. She'd been drawn to Sonny like a magnet. He seemed to have it all, the things she'd been searching for all her life—big successful law firm, money, a place at the top of society, good looks. She basked in his attention, thrilled when he offered a job working for him come work for him and even more excited when he started asking her out.

Before she knew it, he'd asked her to marry him and insisted she move into his house. She was ecstatic, thinking she'd plucked the gold ring from the merry-go-round. But when her new role turned into a tool for him to woo clients and polish his image, she realized that once again her antenna had been off and she'd made a mistake. If only she'd known what was hiding behind that public mask and the hell she was descending into. By that time, however, she'd been trapped, desperate to find a way out.

Especially when she discovered his anger had a brutal side to it.

Of course, it wasn't as if she had the best history when it came to picking men. She'd begun to think there was something wrong with her, that men who either cheated on her or left her hanging were the ones she seemed drawn to. Good looks, smooth personalities, a sense of power—those had been on her unconscious to-do list. At least the others hadn't had anger issues.

Now here she was, lucky she wasn't already dead, and wondering how Drea thought someone could sneak her out of the city without a trace. And then what? Sonny had a history of getting rid of people who could do damage to him. Could Drea's brother protect her from that?

She was lying there trying to will the pain away and ignore the swelling in her left eye when Drea came back into the room with something folded under one arm and slid the glass door closed. She set a little pill cup on the nightstand, pulled the lone chair up to the bed, and leaned close.

"Okay, my friend, it's all set. Zane will be here in fifteen minutes. In a second I'm going to give you this pill to help the pain. Rick won't give you a shot because it would knock you out too much, but he's getting enough meds to take with you for the next couple of days."

Lainie tried not to get too excited. She might actually be getting out of here and away without Sonny's knowledge?

"Your brother will do it?"

Drea nodded. "He's a very good guy, and he'll keep you safe. This is going to work, Lainie. I want you to listen to me. I cleared it with Rick and Maggie. As far as anyone will know, you said you were leaving and that was that. We can't prevent you from doing that. The only way we could stop you is if you had psychiatric problems."

Lainie sighed. "Some people might say that's my problem. Otherwise ,why would I have stayed with Sonny all this time?" She looked up at Drea. "And thank you for not asking."

"That's because in my illustrious career as a nurse I have too often seen how one person can exert control over another so insidiously the chance to leave is gone before the person realizes it."

"So, you *do* understand. Thank god."

Lainie nodded and held up a pair of scrubs. "This is your exit wardrobe. You'll merely be another ED employee to anyone who sees you. We keep extras of these around here in case patients' clothes get ruined or whatever. And I managed to snag a set. We're so busy today no one's going to give you a second look anyway." She held up an employee badge and waved it in front of Lainie. "One of the idiot orderlies dropped this somewhere so, lucky me, I found it and can attach it to your clothing."

Lainie looked at her friend. "I don't know how to thank you. Even after I walked away from our friendship—"

"As far as anyone up here will know, you got up and walked out of here. You weren't forced. Period. Sonny Fitzgerald won't be able to prove any different. And speaking of walking, you'll have to move semi-decently until we get out of here. Can you do that?"

"I'll make myself do it," Lainie answered, her voice fierce. She wasn't going to blow this one chance.

"Good. Take this pill first. It usually starts to work at once and will dull the pain enough to help you move. Come on. Let's get you into scrubs. Then we're going to get you to a back entrance where my brother will pick you up. I know where all the security cameras are to avoid them. We only have to get to a rear door. Can you do it?"

Laine nodded. "I can do anything to get me away from him."

"All right, girlfriend. Let's get it done. Here. Take this pill."

Lainie swallowed the meds then let Drea help her into the scrubs. Was this really going to work?

WHEN HIS CELL PHONE RANG, Zane Halstead was standing in the living room of his month-to-month apartment checking to make sure he hadn't left anything behind. The furniture was rented, so nothing to worry about there. This morning he'd packed up the truck with everything he owned, which wasn't all that much, and he was in the middle of doing one last check.

Renting a place in Tampa near his sister hadn't been a much better idea than going home to the horse farm his folks owned in Ocala. He'd been far from ready to leave the SEALs, and dealing with the injuries that forced him out wasn't helping. He'd gone to the VA hospital here like the doctors at Walter Reed had ordered and tried to do what he was supposed to. After weeks of physical therapy, his arm and hip were as good as they were going to get, but that wasn't enough to keep him with the Teams. When that last mission had gone to shit, and he'd been badly wounded, he'd known his days in the service were numbered. But knowing it and dealing with it were two different things.

Dr. Andrew Ryan, the shrink they'd sent him to, wasn't half bad. He'd recently transferred to the VA hospital in Tampa from another posting and seemed to know more than most what Zane was going through.

"You need a new purpose," he kept telling him. "There are plenty out there."

Yeah, right. The problem was finding one that was the right fit.

He really had no idea what he was going to do next. He'd never developed a serious relationship, so he had no woman waiting to help him rebuild his life. His most marketable skill was identifying and killing bad guys. He knew some former SEALs had gone to work for security agencies but, for whatever reason, that hadn't appealed to him. So, he'd hung around doing not much of anything, driving himself nuts and wondering what he was going to do with the rest of his life and how he'd fit into society. And then he got *The Email*, from Alex Rossi, sheriff of a small county at the foothills of the Crazy Mountains.

The only thing he knew about that area was that another former SEAL, Hank Patterson, had built a security agency out there called Brotherhood Protectors. All the agents were former military, mostly SEAL. Despite the fact that a friend had highly recommended them, he still had no interest in that kind of situation. So, what did the local sheriff want with him?

He clicked on the link to open the email.

Don't delete this before you read it. I'm a former SEAL myself, and rebuilding the sheriff's office here. Long story. Like you, I wasn't sure what to do with myself after the Teams, and I was lucky to land this job, even though the place is a mess. I'm hoping I can talk you into at least a trip out here to look the area over. You might find a new purpose, even if it's nothing more than raising horses, which are in high demand. I hear you're very good with horseflesh. There's a house on six acres you can use rent free while you look the place over. It comes with two horses that need a caretaker soon. If you're interested, my phone number's beneath my signature. Give me a call. It's my cell, so I answer all the time.

Alex Rossi.

Zane thought it was the craziest thing he'd ever seen or heard. This guy contacting him out of the blue like this? But the more he looked at the email, the more he thought, Why the fuck not? He wasn't doing himself or anyone else much good hanging around in his own private pity party. Maybe a change of scenery would do him some good. If he didn't like it, he didn't have to stay. Right? And maybe, away from his family who tiptoed around him, and his friends who treated him as damaged goods, he might actually find a life again. Maybe.

The first thing he did was an Internet search for the man, stunned at what he saw. Alex Rossi had been appointed sheriff by the county commissions when the previous sheriff had been sent to prison, and for a horrendous reason. A group of uber wealthy men for twenty years had made a game of raping young teenage girls, always approaching from behind so their identity was concealed. Threatening death if they reported it, on the chance that a victim might have some clue as to who they were.

Apparently the former sheriff had been paid off to overlook things. Worse than that, to let the men know when a girl had enough courage to report it. It seemed Sheriff Alex Rossi had cleaned up the mess and made sure the men were punished. But what really stuck out was the fact that Bill Schroder, Rossi's father-in-law, was a member of the wealthy elite participating over the years in the rapes. A situation in which Micki, unbeknownst to her father, had been a victim when she was fifteen. And that her father been killed to shut him up. It had been Alex's big case right after he came on the job.

The information that made his head spin was the fact that after the killer was arrested and half the sheriff's deputies fired, Alex turned around and married Micki Schroeder. Knowing all of this he couldn't wait to meet this woman who had survived a rape, the knowledge that her father belonged to the group, was murdered by them, and survived it all to marry the sheriff. Apparently she'd also supported him in the restructuring of his office and setting a new tone for it. A man certainly couldn't ask for a better leader.

The thirty-minute phone call gave him a good feeling about the man and, an hour, later he had agreed to the crazy idea—crazy like the mountains? — said he'd stay in the house, and set about informing his family. It was a testament to how concerned they were about him that neither his parents nor his sister tried to talk him out of it. Well, maybe he'd figure out the rest of his life in Montana and everyone, including himself, could breathe again.

He was getting ready to walk out for the last time when his phone rang. The readout had his sister's name on it.

"Drea? What's up? Aren't you at work?"

"I am, but Zane? I really, really need your help. And please don't say no until you hear it all. Okay?"

"Jesus, girl. What have you gotten yourself into now?"

He listened while she laid out her story for him, especially Lainie Taggert's condition and why her fear of Sonny Fitzgerald was so intense. As she outlined the plan, his stomach knotted, and his fingers tightened their hold on the phone.

"You're kidding me, right? This is a joke to yank my chain."

"No, it isn't." Her voice was low. "I'm dead serious. Dead, by the way, being what this woman will be if we don't pull this deception off and sneak her out of Tampa. Please, Zane. She has no place else to turn. "

He wanted more than anything to say no, but it wasn't who he was. He knew this last-minute call from Drea might screw up his plans. He also knew she wouldn't ask unless she was desperate. Take a strange woman to Montana with him to a situation he wasn't even sure would work? What the hell?

What was he supposed to do with her when he

got there? If she was as banged up as Drea said, she'd need medical care, and he had no idea what kind was available in the sparsely populated area where he was headed.

And what about her? If she was running from an abusive relationship, she was probably terrified of men. He'd seen that before. It always made his blood boil, wondering how a man could treat a woman that way. But she had to be scared shitless, and what would make her trust him? Did she know Drea well enough for that?

Plus, he'd have to find a way to take care of her on the trip. Then, when they got to Montana, he'd have to figure out what to do with her. Hopefully, Drea would have some kind of update for him by then. He needed to know things like how long he was expected to hide Lainie away. Where she would go from there. How she'd get her life together.

Fuck. This wasn't what he needed. He could hardly keep himself together, just taking things one day at a time. But he knew in his heart he'd do that. He was a protector by nature.

"Anything else I should know?"

"Yes. This guy is one mean bastard, and Lainie says she knows something he'd kill her to keep secret."

Fucking great.

He swallowed a sigh.

"You know I can't turn you down, but I'm leaving

in five minutes. Can you get her to that exit by the time I get there?"

"Yes. Yes, yes, yes. Oh, and you'd better bring plenty of cash. If he somehow finds out she's with you, he can track your credit cards."

Jesus! What next?

"Okay. No sweat."

"And, Zane? Thank you so much."

He carried the last of his bags down to the truck and stowed them in the back seat. Then he placed his Glock .9mm in the console along with a box of ammo. Finally, he made sure the knife he always carried was securely strapped to his ankle. He didn't know if this asshole would suddenly show up or what, but, like every other SEAL, he wanted to always be prepared. Then he climbed into the driver's seat and pulled out of his parking space.

What the fuck have I gotten myself into?

He talked to himself all the way to the bank where he pulled out a wad of cash, and then all the way to the hospital, calling himself ten kinds of fool for getting mixed up in this. He could barely take care of himself, let alone someone else who probably needed constant attention.

Fifteen minutes later, Zane pulled up to the delivery door at the hospital, hopped out of his truck, and opened the passenger door. In a moment, a back door to the hospital opened and Drea stepped out, looking both ways before motioning to someone. A guy in scrubs and a white coat, probably the doctor she'd told him about, exited carrying a woman in his arms. As he placed her gently in the passenger seat and buckled her in, Zane took a good look at her, and acid washed in his throat at what he saw.

"We managed to get her dressed and got her out of there without anyone asking questions," Lanie told him, "and we. I also gave her a pain pill, so she's a little out of it."

"What's with the scrubs?"

"So we could walk her through the department and down here without anyone asking questions. I think, though, she's done for. The meds will pretty much knock her out for a while."

Drea had been right about the bruises, the black eye, everything, only she hadn't been quite descriptive enough. Sonny Fitzgerald had most definitely used this woman as a punching bag. Her auburn hair hung limp, and her delicate features were pinched with pain, but even beneath all that he saw a delicate beauty. He wanted to find the man and show him what SEALs did to abusers.

He was sure without the damage she was a knock-out. Not that it mattered right now. She was in desperate need, and he hadn't been with a woman in nearly a year. Wasn't even sure he'd know how to deal with one under normal circumstances.

"Jesus, Drea. She's a mess. Can she even do anything for herself? I don't—"

"It will be fine," Drea insisted. "She's stronger than she looks. I trust you to do whatever is necessary. Figure it out, or she's a dead woman."

"Who is this guy, anyway?"

"Rich and powerful. Do a search on him when you stop for the night." She leaned into the truck and shook the woman gently. "Lainie? Lainie, this is my brother, Zane. He's going to take good care of you, like I said. He's getting you out of here before you can get hurt again."

Lainie's eyes had a wild, frightened look in them as she scanned the area, taking everything in. "S-Sonny?"

"Not here," Drea assured her. "But we want to get you out of here before he decides to show up. This is my brother, Zane. Remember? He's going to take good care of you. He's the best protection you can get. I promise."

Zane thought he could only hope that would be the truth. He stood close to Lainie but didn't touch her, noticing how she shrank away from him. All he wanted as for her to become familiar with his presence.

Lainie wet her lips and stared a moment, as if trying to absorb it all. "Drea's brother?"

He nodded. "And I'll be doing my best to keep you safe."

She swallowed. "And thank you."

"We're gonna get going in a second here, Lainie."

He pitched his voice low, hoping it sounded reassuring. "I want to make sure you're comfortable in the seat and that your seat belt is fastened."

She nodded, not saying a word, but he saw pain etched on her face.

He had to bite down on the pain in his arm when he moved her at a bad angle and did his best not to groan as he settled her. Maybe he should double up on his exercises if he was going to be carting this woman around. She didn't need some gimp for a protector. He swallowed the bitterness, closed the door, and turned to Drea.

"I'm fine," he assured his sister when he saw the look of concern on her face. "It's the truth. I can take good care of her."

"I know you can. I—" She shook her head. "Yes, you're fine. And thank you again for doing this."

"You're welcome."

Handed him a plastic bag with some meds in it plus a plain envelope.

"What's this?" He frowned as he looked at them.

"Her medications for a couple of days plus instructions on how to care for her injuries. There's money in the envelope. She had it with her when she got to the hospital. Apparently, she's been hiding it away for a while. She asked me to give it to you to help pay for the trip."

Zane tried to give it back. "I don't want or need her money."

Drea nodded. "I told her that, but she's going to need some clothing and personal items, since she has nothing with her. You can use some of it for that. I put a note in to let you know what. You can grit your teeth and do it," she insisted when he frowned. "She's in no condition to shop."

"Jesus, Drea." He put the meds inside the truck console and stuffed the envelope into his pocket. "Anything else?"

"One more thing." Drea took a cell phone from her pocket and handed it to him along with the sim card. "It's Lainie's. I turned it off and pulled the sim card and the battery, but you need to get rid of it. I didn't want to do it here at the hospital. You know, just in case. I never know how these things can be traced."

"Will do." He nodded. "I'll text you from the road and let you know how it's going."

"Thank you again, Zane." She gave him a tight hug. "Thank you, thank you, thank you. You're the best brother in the world."

"Yeah, thanks for being a lifesaver," the doctor added.

Zane nodded once, climbed into the truck, and pulled away from the building. Evasion was one of the many things he'd learned as a SEAL, and he didn't trust that this Sonny Fitzgerald asshole wasn't already lurking someplace with his henchmen waiting to see if this woman made a break for it. She certainly couldn't do it without help, so he might be scoping out the area already, despite what Drea said.

He didn't hit Interstate 75 right away, on the off chance someone was on their tail, although he didn't see how that was possible. Drea had accomplished the whole process slick as grease. He drove a few miles on Interstate 4, doubled back, and drove through a couple of busy neighborhoods before he actually headed out of town. When he was satisfied there was no one on his tail, he drove to a street with many warehouses, some of them vacant. Behind one of them, he got out of the car, dropped her cell to the ground, and crushed it beneath his heel. Next was the battery. The remnants went into a trash barrel. Then he headed out of the city, north on Interstate 75 toward Chattanooga. From there he'd head west.

He glanced over at Lainie, bundled into a hospital blanket and scrunched against the door. Somehow, he'd have to find a way for her to trust him, even for a little while.

ABOUT DESIREE HOLT

USA Today best-selling and award-winning author **Desiree Holt** writes everything from romantic suspense and contemporary on a variety of heat levels up to erotic, a genre in which she is the oldest living author. She has been referred to by *USA Today* as the Nora Roberts of erotic romance, and is a winner of the EPIC E-Book Award, the Holt Medallion and a Romantic Times Reviewers Choice nominee. She has been featured on *CBS Sunday Morning* and in *The Village Voice, The Daily Beast, USA Today, The (London) Daily Mail, The New Delhi Times* and numerous other national and international publications.

Desiree loves to hear from readers.

www.facebook.com/desireeholtauthor
www.facebook.com/desiree01holt
Twitter @desireeholt
Pinterest: desiree02holt
Google: https://g.co/kgs/6vgLUu
www.desireeholt.com

www.desiremeonly.com

Follow Her On:

Amazon
https://www.amazon.com/Desiree-Holt/e/
B003LD2Q3M/ref=sr_tc_2_0?qid=1505488204&
sr=1-2-ent

Signup for her newsletter
http://eepurl.com/ce7DeE

facebook.com/desiree01holt
twitter.com/desireeholt

BROTHERHOOD PROTECTORS

ORIGINAL SERIES BY ELLE JAMES

ABOUT ELLE JAMES

ELLE JAMES also writing as MYLA JACKSON is a *New York Times* and *USA Today* Bestselling author of books including cowboys, intrigues and paranormal adventures that keep her readers on the edges of their seats. With over eighty works in a variety of sub-genres and lengths she has published with Harlequin, Samhain, Ellora's Cave, Kensington, Cleis Press, and Avon. When she's not at her computer, she's traveling, snow skiing, boating, or riding her ATV, dreaming up new stories. Learn more about Elle James at www.ellejames.com

Website | Facebook | Twitter | GoodReads | Newsletter | BookBub | Amazon

Follow Elle!
www.ellejames.com
ellejames@ellejames.com

facebook.com/ellejamesauthor
twitter.com/ElleJamesAuthor